My Dad Is Definitely NOT a CRIME LORD

Written by Ben Davis

SCHOLASTIC

For Dougie.

My Dad Is Definitely NOT a CRIME LORD

Published in the UK by Scholastic, 2022
Euston House, 24 Eversholt Street, London, NW1 1DB
Scholastic Ireland, 89E Lagan Road, Dublin Industrial Estate, Glasnevin,
Dublin, D11 HP5F

Text © Ben Davis, 2022
Cover illustration © Allen Fatimaharan, 2022

The right of Ben Davis to be identified
as the author of this work has been asserted by him under
the Copyright, Designs and Patents Act 1988.

ISBN 978 0702 31577 0

A CIP catalogue record for this book is available from the British Library.

Printed by CPI Group (UK) Ltd, Croydon, CR0 4YY
Paper made from wood grown in sustainable forests and other controlled
sources.

1 3 5 7 9 10 8 6 4 2

www.scholastic.co.uk

On the other side of the car park from us is something called "the precinct". It's just a chippy, a convenience store, Gino's Café and a hairdresser's in a row. Opposite, there's a one-storey building with a tin roof that is apparently the community centre. We saw a load of old ladies filing in, but I don't know what for.

The estate is surrounded on both sides by dual carriageways, so it's like being penned in by traffic and smog. There's a dingy underpass going under one of them, which leads to a petrol station and a cemetery. Wow. My old house, with its private drive and three bathrooms and carpet that didn't smell of who knows what, was within walking distance of a cinema, a supermarket and a huge park with a skate ramp in it. This place has nothing. What am I supposed to do all summer?

I'm not even allowed to get in touch with my old mates because if the police find out we'll be in trouble. It's a nightmare. Forget a Worry Book, I'm going to need a Worry Library.

Dad went off for his first day at work this morning. He's been given a job in a dog food factory on the other side of town. He moaned like hell about it when they told him, but it's either that or prison. Tough decision.

He has to be up at seven o'clock to catch the bus. I've never seen him up that early before. Ever. With his old – well, I guess you could call it a job – he kind of got to pick his own hours. He'd usually be in bed when we went to school, then when we got back he'd be gone, not returning home until late.

Having walked around the cemetery, which took ages because Millie insisted on making us read out the names on every headstone she could see, we head back through the underpass, which smells so bad I have to hold my breath, and back to the estate.

"See? It's not so bad," says Mum.

"I appreciate the effort, Mum," I say. "Really, I do. But you know as well as I do, this place sucks."

"Damia—*Finn!*" she says. "Mind your language in front of your sister."

"Sucks! Sucks! Sucks!" Millie yells, jumping up and down in a puddle of what I hope is rainwater.

I hear a laugh coming from an alley. I turn around and there's this kid leaning against the wall. "All right?" he says, in that weird accent they have around here.

We stop. I'm at least relieved that the heat is off me. "Hello, there," says Mum. I struggle to place her tone for a second until I realize it's that same one she used when we first arrived at the flat. Cheerful, but forcing it.

"Ain't seen you before," says the kid, walking towards us. He's about my age, with a shaved head and a wide smile.

"We just moved in," says Mum, doing her posh phone voice for some reason. "What's your name?"

"Colt," he says, with a big sniff.

Mum gently pushes me forward. "This is my son, Finn." She looks proud of herself for getting it right this time. "He's going to be starting at the school this September. Do you go there?"

"Sometimes," says Colt.

Mum laughs, but I can tell it's an *I hope he's joking* kind of thing. "And what year will you be in?"

"Ten," says Colt.

"What a coincidence, so will Finn," says Mum, still pushing me. "You two should have a chat."

"Mum," I moan, quietly.

"Mum, nothing," she says. "Why don't you stay here with Colt while Millie and I go on to the playground." She nods at a clapped-out looking slide and broken swing over by the shops.

"Yeah, come on, Finn," says Colt. "I'll show you around."

It looks like I'm not getting out of this. Still, I don't have any choice about anything else, so why not hang around with some random kid I've just met?

I go over to him and even though I'm not looking, I know Mum is smiling after me like I've just graduated from Brainiac university with a first class degree.

"Sorry about her," I say to Colt. "She's kind of embarrassing."

Colt walks down the alley as if I'm supposed to follow him, so I do. He's wearing a blue T-shirt about two sizes too big for him and his left trainer's sole flaps with every step. They're either third generation hand-me-downs or he found them in a bin. It briefly occurs to me that he could be a murderer and might be taking me to a disused warehouse to pull my guts out through my nose, but I try not to dwell on it.

"Right," says Colt. "Let's get on with the tour, yeah?"

"There's no need," I say. "We've already been for a walk. I think we've seen pretty much everything."

Colt stops and turns around. It's only now I notice all the little scars on his scalp; there's one on his forehead, too. "Yeah, you might have been for a walk," he says, "but you haven't had the real tour."

"OK…" I say.

"Example!" Colt holds up a finger, then twirls it around at the little courtyard we're standing in. Well, *courtyard* might be a bit grand. It's more a patch of weed-riddled concrete and a few garages. "Do you know you are standing on the very spot that I single-handedly took down ten of the hardest blokes in town?"

I laugh, but Colt doesn't.

"What's so funny?" he says.

"Nothing," I say. "I thought you were joking, that's all."

"What, so you don't think I could do it?" he says. That smile he had for Mum is gone completely. His eyes are dead, and it reminds me of Uncle Shane so I have to look away.

"Course not," I say. "You could definitely beat up ten blokes."

Colt purses his lips and nods. "I'm trained in the ancient Japanese art of Daikatana."

I don't have time to ask what Daikatana is supposed to be, because he's already moving on to the next part of the tour. It's the little car park behind the community centre. "This is where we have our Daikatana meetings," he says.

"In there?" I say, nodding through a window

where the old ladies we saw earlier are doing some kind of cowboy dance.

"Nah, out here," Colt says. "In the car park. They don't let us do it in there. Too dangerous." He sniffs, then gobs on the floor.

"So, how many people are in the group?" I ask.

"Two," he says.

"And who is the other member?"

"You," says Colt.

"Oh."

Colt smiles and when he does, the deadness lifts from his eyes and he looks mischievous and fun. "Want your first lesson?"

Not really.

"Um, yeah, OK."

Colt squares up to me. "Try and hit me," he says.

I gulp. "I don't really want to."

This is all new to me. Back home, no one would dare try anything like this with me, not even messing about like this. Not that I'm some kind of hard man or anything. Everyone knew I was a Butcher and that was enough. Being a Jacobs means diddly-squat and I don't like it.

"Nah, go on, I can take it," Colt says, that grin not leaving his face.

I glance over at the playground in the hope that Mum will come and rescue me, but they've gone. Millie probably got bored of going up and down the same slide.

"Hit me," Colt says, his voice threatening this time.

I take a deep breath, then aim a soft, slow-motion punch at his face. Colt grabs my fist and twists it around.

"Ow!" Pain shoots up my arm and my head throbs with anger.

"Who do you think you are? I'm a But—" I stop before I can finish the word.

"You're a boot?" says Colt.

I sigh, my fury settling down into embarrassment. "Yeah."

Then Colt draws his other hand back and swings at me, stopping a millimetre before the end of my nose.

"Daikatana," he whispers.

I take a moment to go through all the things that had to go wrong in my life to lead me to this moment. I mean, Daikatana? What's the matter with him?

"That was lesson one, Finn, but there'll be more," says Colt. "Right, on to the next part of the tour."

"Oh, actually I need to go," I say. "My sister

needs help with…" I search my brain for something believable but come back empty-handed. *Thanks, brain. Excellent work.* "My sister needs help."

Colt laughs. A single bark. "BAH! Family, eh? I got a sister, too. And a brother, but we don't talk about him."

"Oh," I say. "Why's that?"

"I said we don't talk about him," he snaps. "Now come on, Finn."

I follow him, even though I really don't want to, to the bridge over the dual carriageway on the other side of the estate.

"So this is it," says Colt.

"A bridge?" I say.

Cars whizz past us, kicking up freshly dropped litter.

"Not just any bridge." Colt smiles. "Come on."

He turns and runs up the steps, taking them two at a time. The sun is peeking out from behind the clouds, and I'm beginning to regret wearing my hoodie. I'm beginning to regret leaving the flat in the first place.

There is a railing about the height of my shoulder running along the main walkway of the bridge. I look down and it makes my stomach do that top-of-the-roller-coaster lurch.

"This is the best place in the whole estate," Colt says.

He leans on the railings and looks down at the traffic speeding under us.

"Why's that, then?" I ask.

Colt taps the side of his head. "It's where I get all my thinking done."

Up to this point, Colt didn't strike me as one of life's big thinkers, but I don't say anything. I didn't want to get chucked off and squished by a ten-tonne lorry.

"It's good to just watch the cars and wonder where they're going," he says. "Like that Merc in the fast lane. I bet he's going to a business meeting. And see that green Skoda? Probably off to a garden centre or somewhere like that."

My heart sinks. Is this what passes for fun around here? If my old mates could see me now, they'd die laughing. Colt nudges me. "How about that Punto? Where's that going?"

I watch the silver car disappear into the distance. How am I supposed to know where it's going? I shrug. "McDonalds?"

"Yeah," says Colt, his eyes wide. "Yeah, maybe

they're getting a Big Mac meal each. Large. With milkshakes. And extra chicken nuggets!" He looks like he's about to drool. How long has it been since he's had a McDonalds?

"I've really got to go now, Colt," I say.

Colt shakes his head like he's waking himself up. "But there are loads more things to show you!"

"Show me some other time, yeah?" I say.

Colt sighs and he stuffs his hands in the pockets of his tracksuit bottoms. "All right. See you tomorrow."

Tomorrow? That's what you think, mate. I'm avoiding you for the rest of the summer. For the rest of my LIFE.

Worry Book

What if Colt murders me?

CHAPTER 4

Me and Millie are in the lounge trying to watch Millie's favourite show, *Amazing Kids*, on the pathetically small TV. As the title suggests, it's about kids who do so-called AMAZING stuff. It's hosted by this shouty, bouncy guy with big hair called Casey Kellman who keeps yelling "Booyeah!". It bores the pants off me, but Millie never lets me change the channel.

So now I'm passing the time by staring at the wall. If you relax your eyes, the pattern on the wallpaper kind of looks like a load of bear heads staring back at you. *Hello, Wall Bears. I think I'm going to be spending a lot of time with you this summer.*

The front door flies open with a bang and Dad stomps in.

"Hello, Daddy!" Millie yells. "Did you have fun at work?"

Dad pats Millie on the head and goes straight through to the kitchen, where Mum is making dinner.

"Seriously?" he says.

"Everything all right, love?" says Mum.

"I have just finished my first day at work," he says. "Then I have to sit on a stinking bus, and I get home and, what's this? No dinner."

"It'll be ready in five minutes," says Mum.

I hear Dad sigh. "Fine. Sorry for snapping. Stressful day."

I begin to relax a little. Sometimes Dad just has a little outburst, and then he's fine. He comes back into the lounge and sits heavily in the chair, where he lands with a thud. I made that mistake, too. These chairs don't have as much bounce as our old ones and it's easy to forget. Dad grunts under his breath, snatches up the TV remote and navigates to the sports channel.

"Daddy! I was watching *Amazing Kids*!" Millie moans, but Dad ignores her.

The screen goes black and a little box pops up.

You do not have access to this channel. See our
website to upgrade.

Dad throws the remote down, smashing the back off and sending the batteries scattering across the floor. Apart from the sound of Mum dishing up the dinner as fast as she can, it's silent.

We sit quietly around the tiny kitchen table. One of the legs is short and Mum had to wedge a folded-up leaflet underneath to stop it wobbling. We've got shepherd's pie and it's really good. Dad finishes his, then puts down his knife and fork and rubs his forehead.

"Sorry for before, guys," he says. "It's just that job."

"What's wrong?" Mum asks quietly.

"All I do all day is check cans for damages and put them in boxes. Check, box, check, box, check, box."

"That sounds boring," says Millie.

Dad smiles, reaches across the table and squeezes her hand. "It is, Mils. And it's not only that. I've got this supervisor. He's only a kid, barely out of school, and he's ordering me about like I'm a joke." Dad blinks hard. "I'm not a joke."

"We know you're not," says Mum. "Just do your best. That's all you can do."

Dad sighs. "You're right," he says. "This is a new start – but it's going to take some getting used to."

CHAPTER 5

"Finn!" Mum calls from the lounge. I'm lying on my bed, counting my teeth with my tongue. I was just getting on to the bottom row and Mum shouting has made me lose count.

"What?" I yell back.

"Your friend is here to see you!"

Friend? What friend? For a hopeless second, I think Freddie or Conor or, heck, even Will from my old school might have somehow found me. I jump out of bed and run in there, but when I see who it is, I want to turn back.

"All right, Finn!" says Colt, the dents in his head looking even deeper thanks to the buzzing light strip above him on the landing outside.

"Oh," I say. "Hello."

"You up for carrying on with the tour?" he says.

Mum smiles. "Well, isn't that lovely? Go on. It's a beautiful day. You should be out there, enjoying it."

I grudgingly go with Colt. He nudges me in the ribs as we walk down the stairs. "Bet you're wondering how I knew where you lived," he says.

"Kind of."

Colt shrugs, still smiling. "Ampleforth is just that kind of place. When new people move in, everyone talks about it."

Seems weird to me. Back where we used to live, nobody cared. Everyone just kept to themselves. We had friends, sure, but they were mainly Dad's friends. When it came to our road, though, the houses were so big and spaced-out, you could rent your spare room out to a three-headed alien from Jupiter and no one would know.

"Right, I'll introduce you to the lads," he says as we round the corner.

"What lads?"

He doesn't answer. Ahead of us, hanging around in the playground are two more boys our sort of age. They both have black hoodies on with the hoods pulled up, even though it's a warm day.

"This is Finn, the new kid," says Colt, karate

chopping my arm, which is really annoying. "Finn, this is Jay and Dylan."

I say hello, but they don't respond. The bigger one, who I think is Dylan, aims a kick at the broken swing. The other one comes closer. He narrows his eyes like he's inspecting me. "Say something else," he says.

"What do you mean?" I say, stepping back a little.

"Anything," he says.

"Um … morning? My name's Finn?" I say. Wow. Why has this place turned me into such a dork?

He nods like he's worked something out. "You do sound different. You're not from round here, are you?"

I freeze. They gave us clear instructions about things like this. We're supposed to lie and tell people we're from Atherworth, a town about five miles away, so that's what I do.

"He don't sound like he's from Atherworth," says Jay, his little eyes darting around.

Colt jumps at him and grabs him in a headlock. "I've been left with no choice but to take you down, Jay," he says. "No one gives my new mate a hard time and gets away with it."

Jay hits Colt in the ribs with a few jabs and soon

they're rolling around on the floor, wrestling while me and Dylan watch, awkwardly.

"Is this that Daikatana, then?" I ask Dylan.

Dylan gawps at me like I've just asked him to explain the theory of relativity. "Wha'?"

Colt jumps to his feet and hits me with another karate chop, this time harder. "We don't talk about that around others," he says. "Right, come on."

What's he talking about? Others? Does that mean I'm the only one he's shown Daikatana to? Why? Does he think I need to learn it because I'm a wuss?

Colt leads on, with the rest of us following behind. "We're taking him to that place they found that geezer."

Dylan and Jay chuckle darkly.

"What geezer?" I ask, but no one answers.

They lead me to this concrete trench on the other side of the estate, opposite a row of houses. At the far end, there's a grate. I guess it's to collect rainwater or something, but right now it's bone dry, baked by the sun.

"It was down here where they found him," says Colt.

"Found who?" I say, starting to get nervous.

"The *geezer*," says Colt.

"What happened?"

"He crossed Ronnie," says Jay, then nudges me hard with his shoulder, almost making me fall in the trench.

"Who's Ronnie?" I say.

"Ronnie runs things around here," says Colt. "You can't do anything without Ronnie saying it's OK."

Hearing that brings back memories of things I heard about Dad and Uncle Shane. I have to shake my head to stop myself thinking about them. Some things need to stay buried.

It's quiet. Somewhere on the estate someone is playing loud music, but it just sounds like a low hum from here.

"Hey, look at him!" Dylan points at a kid sitting at the other end of the trench. His legs are dangling and it looks like he's reading a massive book.

Colt smiles, that same one he always seems to flash when he wants to turn on the charm. This time, though, there's something in his eyes I don't like.

"OI!" he yells as he approaches the boy. Jay nudges me again, encouraging me to follow, so I do.

The boy looks different. I don't just mean because he's Black and the vast majority of people on this estate aren't. It's not just his clothes, either:

a neat button-down shirt and pressed trousers like you might wear to a party. It's something else; I can't figure it out yet. He sighs and lays his book in his lap.

"What you reading, Tag?" says Colt.

"My name is Tel," says the boy. "You know it is."

His voice is definitely different. It's smooth, and, well, posh. He sounds like he should do voice-overs for butter adverts.

"Answer the question," Dylan grunts.

Tel briefly locks eyes with me, like he's registered a new arrival, then looks back at the others and holds up the giant book. It's probably getting on for a thousand pages long and the front cover says, *Philosophy: A Beginner's Guide.*

Dylan laughs. He reads the title out loud, but he pronounces it as "fill a Sophie". "What does that mean?" he asks.

Tel's jaw tightens. I can tell this isn't the first time he's had to explain himself to these three. "Philosophy." He corrects Dylan, firmly. "It is the study of existence."

"That sounds well interesting, mate," says Colt in an over-friendly, mocking way. "Why don't you tell us all about it?"

Tel slowly looks at all of us in turn, then back at Colt. If he's intimidated, he's hiding it really well.

"OK," he says. "Well, let's start off with a proposition. Something like, 'Colton is a moron.'"

"Oi!" says Jay.

"Now, someone like Plato would say that our perception of reality lies in our minds, so Colton is not objectively a moron, he just is in my mind. And likely the minds of everyone else."

The three of them step closer, looming over him.

"On the other hand," Tel goes on, unperturbed, "an aestheticist would want to question it further. What is a moron? Why is Colton a moron? What is it about Colton that makes him so moronic?"

"Watch your mouth," Colt warns.

"You asked," says Tel. "I'm just explaining things in a way you might understand. Now, I'm going to mention one more philosophical theory: absolutism. This is the most appropriate one in this situation. In absolutism, there is no debate: Colton is a moron."

Colt grabs the collar of Tel's shirt and drags him to his feet. "You need to learn when to shut up."

I should do something about this, shouldn't I? This isn't right. But what can I do? The only weapon I ever had in my arsenal was my name. Without that, I've got nothing. Besides, Colt knows where I live. Who knows what he's capable of?

Colt drags Tel to the edge of the trench. It's a drop of over a metre. If he pushes him, he would really get hurt.

"You want to end up like that geezer?" Colt growls, the other two crowding behind him.

Tel doesn't speak. I look around to see if any adults are nearby, but it's deserted.

"Well, do you?"

It goes quiet again. Then, there's a slapping sound and Colt wheels away, holding his face. Jay tries to grab Tel, but he is tossed to the ground. Dylan swings at him, but Tel ducks and sweeps his legs from under him. He starts towards me, but I hold my hands up in surrender, so he just scoops up his book and runs away.

"We're gonna get you!" Colt screams after Tel, still holding his face. "Trust me! You're finished!"

Worry Book

What are they going to do to this Tel kid?

I don't want to be involved, whatever it is.

CHAPTER 6

Mum and Dad are having an argument, so I've activated standard protocol: bedroom, headphones, pretend it's not happening.

The problem is, now I'm sharing a room with Millie, I'm constantly being interrupted and have to pause the music, which means I'm getting snippets of the argument. It seems to be mainly based around Dad's job. He's complaining that the money he's getting isn't enough. And Mum is asking what happened to all that talk about working hard and getting a promotion, but Dad is acting as if he never said it and blah, blah, blah.

Dad never told me how he earned money before. As I grew older, I got more of an idea, and I heard a few things when the court case was in the news, but I try not to think about it. When I do it makes me feel a bit sick.

What I do know is we never had to worry about money. We always had nice things, went on good holidays: Disney World, fancy hotels with huge swimming pools and room service. Now look at us.

Millie is snuggled up next to me on my bed. "I hate this place," she says.

"Me too."

"I want to go home."

"Me too."

This has become our regular routine. It's almost like we're actors doing the same play every day.

"I don't know how much longer this can go on," says Dad.

"But you haven't even been there a week," says Mum.

"SHUT UP!" Dad almost screams. "SHUT YOUR MOUTH."

Millie lets out a little yelp and nestles into me further. She's shaking. I reach into my drawer and pull out my spare headphones and a splitter. I plug them into my laptop and put them over her ears, then find a playlist of all her favourite annoying kiddy songs and turn them up as loud as she can stand it. This is how it's going to have to be from now on.

Millie starts to cry. I want to cry, too, but I fight it, like I always do, remembering all the times Dad shouted at me, saying things like "Stop crying. You're supposed to be a man." I have to be the strong big brother. The shouting becomes a low, background hum. I close my eyes and try to concentrate on the music, which is a lot easier when it's metal or rap and not "I Wanna Hug a Huggy Bear".

BEEEEEEEWW, BEWBEWBEW.

A piercing alarm cuts through everything. It's so loud, it makes my teeth vibrate.

"What's that?" Millie yells.

Mum opens our bedroom door. I can tell from her face she's been crying. "Come on. Sounds like it's a fire alarm."

We throw our shoes on and, along with everyone else in the block, head down the stairs and out into the car park. The sun is beginning to set, bathing everything in an orange glow that makes it look almost half-decent. Our next-door neighbour, Mr O'Neill, a small man with a white moustache, folds his arms and rolls his eyes. "Looks like someone's burned their sausages again."

Mum smiles a little, but Dad doesn't even acknowledge him, just stares straight ahead.

"Does this happen a lot, then?" I ask Mr O'Neill.

He nods with a helpless smile. "Just be thankful it's a nice evening and not the dead of winter."

"How long do we have to wait before we can go back in?"

"The fire brigade have to come and make sure there's no real fire," he says. "Could be twenty minutes, could be a couple of hours. Depends how busy they are."

Great. So we could be stuck out here for ages. What am I supposed to do? Mum and Dad are standing there like a couple of statues, just waiting to launch back into their argument. What's extra awkward is I'm pretty sure that Mr O'Neill would have heard the whole thing through the super-thin walls.

I notice Mr O'Neill tense up. He looks at the floor, his mouth drawn into a thin half smile. A man is walking past us and everyone is getting out of his way. It's like watching a whale swim into a shoal of fish. The man is big and his bald head shines under the late afternoon light. He wears a black suit with a white shirt open at the top.

Everyone is either looking at him or making a great effort not to. Chat quietens down. There's a look in his eye as he passes. I can't describe it, but it sends a jolt up my spine.

He slowly strides across the car park, gets into the passenger seat of a waiting car and disappears.

As the car pulls away, the atmosphere goes back to normal.

Dad nudges Mr O'Neill. "Who was that, then?"

Mr O'Neill puffs out his cheeks. "That's Ronnie. You're better off staying out of his way."

Wait a second. I've heard that name before. Wasn't Ronnie the guy Colt said ran the estate?

"Oh yeah?" says Dad. I look up at him and his face is clouded over, like his brain is making millions of calculations at the same time. "Why's that, then?"

"He's trouble," says Mr O'Neill, like he doesn't want to say any more than that.

"Right," says Dad, still looking deep in thought.

I sense a presence next to me and, without turning my head, I somehow know who it is.

"I could have taken that Tel kid, you know," Colt says, his voice low. "He just took me by surprise, that's all. Whatever fighting he's trained in is no match for Daikatana."

43

I lead Colt away from Mum and Dad. I don't want them hearing I've been involved in a fight, even if it was only as a bystander. We head over to the fence by the playground. An ice cream man must have heard about the alarm and wanted to cash in, because we're almost drowned out by "The Teddy Bears' Picnic".

"Me and the boys have been talking about our next move," he says.

"What do you mean?"

"Taking down Tel," he says, keeping his voice low.

"But why, though?" I say. "He just seems a bit weird, that's all. Why not just leave him alone?"

Colt glares at me, those eyes like two hot lamps. I feel like a badger about to be mowed down on the dual carriageway. Back in my old life, if I called someone off, that would be it. I did it loads of times. There were times I didn't, too, but let's not even go there.

"Because he made us look like chumps, and he's going to pay," says Colt. "Don't you get it?"

"Yeah," I say, getting nervous and hating every millisecond. "I get it."

"Good," says Colt. "And you're going to help this time."

"What do you want me to do?" I scan the area for an escape and find nothing.

Colt wipes his nose on his sleeve. "I'll tell you when we get there."

I look back at the car park. Everyone from the block is standing around, chatting. I can't see Mum and Dad, but I bet they're not joining in.

"So I take it you've known Tel for a while, then?" I ask.

Colt spits on the floor. "Yeah. He thinks he's too good for this place, always kissing up to teachers and reading. He's got to be reminded where he is; you know what I mean?"

I nod, even though I don't really. Who cares if someone does well at school? Why can't everyone just mind their own business?

"Yeah, I know what you mean," I say. "Anyway, I've got to go."

"Got to go where?" Colt stands in front of me. "You can't go back in your flat. The alarm's still on."

He's got me there. We spend the next hour exactly where we are, with Colt telling me, in excruciating detail, about everyone in our year at school and all the reasons he hates them. When the fire engine pulls into the car park, I feel like running over and hugging them. By now, it's getting dark and a little cooler.

"Look, I'd better go back," I say. "They'll be letting us in any minute."

This time, Colt lets me go. "All right, Finn. You rest up, cos I'll be calling on you soon."

When I get back to the car park, Mum and Dad are still standing in silence. Mum looks at me and smiles, but it soon disappears. "Where's Millie?" she asks.

"What do you mean?" I say. "I left her here with you."

"No, you didn't," says Dad. "She walked off with you and that lad."

I spin around, looking everywhere for Millie, but I can't see her.

"Oh no," Mum whispers. She heads towards the playground and I try to tell her Millie won't be there, but it's like she can't hear me.

"Millie!" she shouts. "Millie, where are you?"

The fire alarm cuts out and people start heading back towards the block. Dad starts shouting, too. Where could she have got to? The sun is dipping behind the block. It will be completely dark very soon.

I try and ignore all the horrifying scenarios playing out in my mind. I see her wandering on to the dual carriageway, or tightrope walking across the railing on the bridge. I see Uncle Shane showing up and … and I don't even want to think about that.

"MILLIE!" I yell. "IF YOU'RE HIDING, THIS REALLY ISN'T FUNNY!"

Mr O'Neill comes over. "Is your little girl missing?"

"Yes!" says Mum, getting frantic. "Have you seen her?"

Mr O'Neill shakes his head. "Hold on, though." He sticks his fingers in his mouth and does a super loud whistle. All the people on their way back into the block stop.

"A little girl has gone missing," he shouts over at them. "We need some help finding her."

Everyone comes back. Literally everyone. Mr O'Neill turns to Mum and Dad. "Don't worry, I'll divide everyone into teams, you just get looking."

Mum and Dad move quickly, heading towards the shops. I see Gino from the café running towards the groups. He's seen Millie before so at least he'll know who he's looking for.

The nightmare scenarios keep running through

my brain at a million miles an hour and I'm powerless to stop them. For a whole hour, no one knew where she was. She could be anywhere.

I run to the bridge, but there's no sign of her there. Then I sprint to the other side of the estate and look in the underpass but it's empty.

This can't be happening. I want to cry, but I don't have time. I have to find Millie. The street lights have clicked on. The sky is a deep purple.

All around the estate, I hear people calling out for Millie.

"Where are you, love?"

"Come out, there's a good girl!"

There's a row of houses up ahead. I'll check them out. For a second I think I see her sitting on an overgrown lawn, but it turns out to be a big doll some kid must have dropped there. I stop and close my eyes, my chest heaving. Where could she be? Where would she even go around here? I try to get inside her head. It's hard because her brain seems to consist entirely of TV and Cherry Zingas, but there must be something. I'm getting so into it; I can almost hear her voice. Wait. Can I hear her voice?

I move quickly and quietly along the row. There it is again. It sounds just like her. And it sounds like it's coming from behind the houses. I run down an alley which leads to a bit of tarmac and a few ramshackle garages and my heart nearly leaps out of my mouth when I see Millie. And she's not alone. She's with someone. Or some*thing*.

CHAPTER 7

The figure is dressed entirely in what looks like black rubber. Black boots, black trousers, black top, black gloves, black mask. On its chest are brilliant white, twinkling stars.

"Millie!" I say. "Come here."

Millie sees me and smiles. "This is my friend," she says. "His name is Star Kid."

"Don't be afraid," says Star Kid in a deep, gravelly, Batman-like voice. "I'm just here to help."

"Come here, Millie," I say again.

Millie stays next to Star Kid. She seems to like him. I can't say I'm so keen. He looks like a massive weirdo.

"Come on, now," I say. "You've got our entire block out looking for you. Mum and Dad are worried sick."

Millie blows a raspberry. "I hate Daddy."

"I know," I say. "But you have to come home."

"That's not home," she says. "I want to go to real home. That's what I was looking for."

I get a lump in my throat the size of a boulder. "Millie, you can't walk there, it's really far away."

"I found her here," says Star Kid.

"Did you know she was missing?" I ask him.

"Of course I did," he says. "I'm a superhero."

I splutter with laughter. "You're a what, now?"

"A superhero," he replies, deadly serious. "I keep the estate safe."

"Well, you're doing a bang-up job," I say, nodding at the ruins of a garage that had clearly burned down at some point.

"I might not stop every incident," says Star Kid, "but I'm coming for all those who want to make this place worse. Including you, if you continue."

"Continue?" I say. "Continue what?"

Star Kid doesn't answer and just stares at me. What does he know?

"Star Kid is my friend," says Millie. "He gave me this." She holds up a toy Santa Claus.

"That's nice," I say. "I mean, it's really unseasonal, but it's nice."

"Star Kid told me to write letters to Santa and put

them next to this toy and Santa will read them," says Millie.

"I'm sure he will," I say. "Now say goodbye. We've got to go back to Mum and Dad."

I grab Millie's hand and gently pull her away.

"These family problems," Star Kid says. "They should be resolved, or this may well happen again."

"All due respect, 'Star Kid'," I say, "but that's none of your business. See you around."

When we get back to the car park, Mum is talking to a police officer, and when she sees us coming, she runs and scoops up Millie.

"Oh, my baby, my baby. Never do that to me again, do you understand?"

I was expecting Dad to be angry, but he isn't. He pulls us all in for a big hug in the car park. Everyone is really happy that Millie has been found safe and well.

"Where did you go?" Mum asks Millie.

"I was walking around, and I got lost and a superhero saved me," she replies.

Mum laughs. Millie is always coming out with random stories like that, and this sounds like it is no different. I'm not about to tell them that some kid really is running around the estate at night pretending to be a superhero.

On the way back up to the flat, Dad digs me in the ribs and nods. I think that's his way of saying he thinks I did a good job and he's proud of me. I'm sure it is.

Worry Book

Millie disappearing is another reminder that Uncle Shane is still out there.

Where is he?

And what's the deal with that Star Kid?

CHAPTER 8

With Dad at work, Mum has taken us out for another so-called "family trip". Is it to Disney World? Is it to the beach? No, it's to Gino's Café.

"Gino asked us to come down for a coffee, so that's what we'll do," says Mum.

"But I don't like coffee," says Millie, clutching her new Santa Claus toy.

Mum squeezes Millie's hand, which I notice she's holding extra tight. "I'm sure there'll be something for you, sweetheart."

Gino's is nicer than I was expecting. It's clean and neat, with black chairs and tables, a shiny wooden counter and pictures of scenes from Italy on the walls. It smells like rich coffee and pastries. When he sees us, he breaks into a huge smile.

"Well, if it isn't my favourite family!" he says.

Mum blushes a little. "Oh, we just thought we'd stop by for a drink. How are you, Gino?"

"All the better for seeing you," he says, with a wink. Then he turns his attention to Millie. "You gave us an awful fright last night, young lady."

Millie presses herself into Mum's side, the way she always does when she gets shy. Gino laughs and rolls his eyes. "Kids, eh?" he says. "Right, what can I get you folks?"

We sit down at a table and Gino brings us over our order: a cappuccino for Mum, an orange juice for me and an apple juice for Millie. Then, with a flourish, he puts down a plate with little pieces of cake and pastries. They look delicious.

"Oh, but we didn't order these," says Mum.

"I know," says Gino. "But I thought after everything that happened last night, you deserved a little treat. These are authentic Italian pastries, just like my grandma used to make." Suddenly he hunches over and pulls a funny face. "Oh, Gino, when-a you gonna find-a yourself a good-a lady?"

Millie laughs and claps. Gino seems to love this and gives a bow. "All right, I'll leave you to it," he says. "Buon appetito!" And with that, he slings his cloth over his shoulder and goes back to the counter, where a couple of old ladies, who are obviously in love with him, are waiting.

"Cake man is funny," says Millie, shoving an iced bun into her mouth.

I notice Mum looking over at the counter. To begin with, I think she's staring at Gino, which would be super weird, but after a couple of seconds, I realize what she's looking at. There's a sign.

HELP WANTED.

COMPETITIVE PAY AND ALL THE SFOGLIATELLE YOU CAN EAT.

APPLY WITHIN.

"You thinking of going for that job?" I ask.

Mum blushes and shakes her head. She probably didn't realize she was being so obvious.

"No," she says. Then she stops and frowns. "I couldn't."

"Why not?" I ask.

Mum seems to be searching for an answer. "Well," she says, "I haven't had a job in years. Besides, what would your dad say?"

I shrug. "He's always moaning about how his job doesn't pay enough. If you had one, wouldn't he be happy?"

When Gino finishes serving the old ladies, he must notice us looking at the sign, because he comes bouncing back over.

"Thinking of applying for the position, eh?" he says to Millie. "Well, I'm flattered, sweetheart, but you're a bit too young." He gently squeezes Millie's shoulder, making her giggle again.

"Mum was thinking about it," I say.

Gino raises an eyebrow. "Is that right?"

"No," says Mum, blushing again. "Well, maybe it might be nice to have something to do, but ... oh, Da— I mean, Finn, you mustn't embarrass me like that."

"We can hold an interview right now, if you like," says Gino. "Question one: how are you at pouring coffee?"

"Really good!" Millie yells.

"Excellent." Gino draws a tick on an invisible clipboard.

"And how about people skills?" he says. "Can you get through a day without telling Edna over there to get stuffed?"

Mum laughs. "I suppose so."

Gino ticks again.

"And one more question: how's your criminal record?" He laughs, but we don't. Mum looks at the table, smiling a little.

When Gino seems to notice his joke hasn't gone over that well, he gets serious. "Look, the job's yours if you want it. It would save me a lot of hassle with recruitment and what have you."

Mum smiles. "But you don't know me," she says gently. "I could be anyone."

Gino chuckles. "I'm a good judge of character. You have an honest face. Now come on, do you want to jump on the Pastry Train or not?"

Mum goes quiet.

"You might be able to get us free cakes!" says Millie.

Gino laughs again. I like his laugh. It's loud and weird but he obviously doesn't care what anyone thinks about it. "This one," he says, pointing at Millie with finger pistols. "I can tell she's going to be a handful."

Mum suddenly perks up. "Ah," she says. "I can't take the job."

"Why?" says Gino, pulling an exaggerated sad face.

"Millie," says Mum. "Finn can take care of himself, but Millie needs me."

Gino rolls his eyes. "You think I hadn't thought of that? There's a day care in the community centre. She'll love it there."

Millie gasps. "Are there toys?"

"Toys?" Gino says. "There are so many toys you can barely move."

"And trikes?" says Millie.

"Like you wouldn't believe," says Gino.

Millie gasps and tugs on Mum's arms. "Please, Mummy, I want to go to the toys and trikes place!"

Mum sighs. I notice the hint of a smile on her lips. "Can I let you know?"

Gino folds his arms. "Fine," he says. "But I can't keep it open for too long. I've got applicants beating down my door."

"Really?" says Mum.

"No," says Gino. "You're the only one. I just wanted to sound like a big shot. Anyway, when you've made up your mind, you know where I am."

Gino goes back to the counter, loudly singing along with the radio.

"You should totally do it," I say, trying not to make it too obvious that I'd just like the flat to myself for a couple of days a week.

"But your dad…"

"What, you have to ask his permission to do *everything*?" I say. "You are your own person, you know."

Oh, empty flat. Oh, TV remote. You are so close.

Mum smiles, properly this time. "You know what? You're right. I'm going to take it. I'd better tell Gino before I change my mind."

I'm sitting on the sofa with Millie. She has been in a great mood all day at the thought of all the toys at the day care. We walked past after we'd been to Gino's and she saw the kids playing outside and wanted to go straight away.

Mum has been tidying the flat for hours. She hasn't sat down since we got in. She's nervous, I can tell. Dinner is ready to be served and on the table at exactly five forty-five, which is when Dad usually comes in. She has put on a playlist of his favourite old man rock songs and everything.

When Dad walks in, I see his mood lift a little. "Now this is what I'm talking about!" he says.

Mum comes in from the kitchen and gives him a hug. "I've made your favourite: chicken curry."

"It smells delicious," says Dad. "It almost makes a day in that hellhole worthwhile."

We sit down at the table while Mum puts our plates down in front of us. We've all got big portions of curry, apart from Millie who seems to only exist on chicken nuggets and chips.

"What have I done to deserve this?" says Dad.

I look at Mum, who's just sat down. "Oh, just felt like treating you, that's all."

Dad narrows his eyes at her, then at me. I can tell he thinks something's up. He stares at us for a little longer before going back to his dinner.

"Daddy," says Millie, through a mouthful of nugget. "I'm going to the toy place next week."

"Really, darling?" says Dad, not looking up from his plate.

"Yep," says Millie. "And I'm going to play with all the other boys and girls."

"OK, Millie," says Mum. "Eat your dinner."

This time, Dad puts his knife and fork down. "What's the matter with you?" he says to Mum.

"Me?" says Mum. "Nothing."

"You're acting jumpy," says Dad. "There's

something off."

I look over at Mum. Her neck has gone all red and blotchy. When is she going to tell him?

"I'm fine," she says.

"Mummy has got a job!" Millie blurts out.

Well, that's done it.

"What are you talking about?" says Dad. "What job?"

Mum takes a deep breath. "We went down to Gino's earlier and he offered me a job."

Dad laughs bitterly. "Oh, I bet he did."

"What's that supposed to mean?" says Mum.

"That sleazeball fancies you," he says.

"He does not," Mum snaps back.

"Why else would he help you move the stuff from the van?" Dad folds his arms and sits back.

"Because it's a nice thing to do?" says Mum, her voice starting to get louder. "Because he could see we were struggling? Because *you* weren't there?"

Dad stops smiling. "Watch it," he says.

"I thought you'd be happy about me taking the job," Mum goes on. "Like Finn says, you're always complaining about money."

Dad turns his attention to me. "Oh, *Finn* said that, did he?" He always emphasizes my new name weirdly.

I can tell he hates it.

"Yes, he did, and I agree with him," says Mum.

Dad stands up from the table, paces a little and sits back down. "But you don't work," he says. "I'm the breadwinner of this family. I always have been, and I always will be."

"And that's fine," says Mum. "But times have changed. You need help."

Dad is beginning to turn red. Millie holds my hand under the table. Here we go. Brace yourself.

Suddenly, like a switch has been flipped, the redness drains away and Dad smiles. "You know what?" he says. "Fine. You go and work at the café."

Oh. Well, that didn't work out how I was expecting.

"Really?" says Mum.

Dad picks his knife and fork back up and jabs at the pieces of chicken on his plate. "Yeah," he says. "Because I know you won't stick it."

This time Mum laughs. "Oh, won't I?"

"I guarantee you," says Dad. "You won't last a month."

Worry Book

The arguments are happening more often.

CHAPTER 9

"See that house over there?" asks Colt, nodding over the road. He called for me again and I couldn't think of a good enough excuse not to go. The house he's referring to is like nothing I've ever seen before. The grass on the front lawn is taller than me and the small bits of the windows that are visible reveal stacks of boxes and papers and who knows what else. It looks abandoned.

"The witch lives there," he says. "Bloody Mary, her name is."

"Really?" I say. I thought witches lived in little wooden houses in the woods, not blocky things with lawns that haven't been mowed since my mum was a baby.

"Totally," says Colt. "When I heard your little sis

had gone missing, I thought the witch had got her. She does that, you see. She eats kids."

I laugh. "If she eats kids, how is she not in prison?"

"Bloody Mary is smart," says Colt, tapping his head. "She leaves no trace behind, so they don't have any evidence against her. Everyone knows she eats kids, though."

We're ambling down a cycle path in the baking heat looking for Tel. Jay and Dylan are a couple of streets away. None of them know where he lives, just that it's on this side. Colt still hasn't told me what he expects me to do. He just keeps hopping from foot to foot and rubbing his hands and saying stuff like, "He's going to wish he never messed with us."

I look back at the so-called witch's house. It seems creepier now. I don't believe there's a crazed cannibal living there, but the idea that anyone could actually live in a house like that weirds me out. You'd have to be pretty weird to put yourself in that situation. Colt's phone buzzes and when he looks at the message, he whoops and smacks me on the shoulder.

"They got him! Let's go!"

Colt takes off along the cycle path. I follow. I don't think I want to, but something in my gut is telling me to go. We end up by that concrete trench where we saw Tel the other day. Colt jumps in, then scrambles to the other side. There is a cluster of thick trees. I can hear voices.

"Where is he?" Colt yells.

"Over here, by the pipe!" I recognize the voice of Jay somewhere, but I can't see him.

We pick our way through the trees. I can see some shapes through the green. As we get closer, I see Jay and Dylan standing over Tel, who is on the floor. I try to ask Colt what they are doing, but he doesn't hear me.

We get to a clearing and when I see what they've done, I feel sick. They have tied Tel's wrist to a thick, rusty metal pipe with a cable. He kicks out at them, but they are standing too far away for him to make impact and they cackle hysterically.

"Look at him!" says Jay. "Flapping around like a dying fish."

"Let me go, you imbeciles," Tel grunts.

"No way," says Dylan. "We're saving you for Colt."

Colt smiles and kneels on the ground. "Hello, mate." His voice is soft and soothing, like he's trying to coax a kitten. "This is a shame, isn't it?"

Tel says nothing, just growls.

That smile won't leave Colt's face. It's like a mask: rigid and unmoving.

"Now, what I want to know is, do you want to say it again?"

"Say what?" says Tel.

Colt chuckles. "You must have a bad memory, mate! You called me a moron, remember? Now, do you want to say it again, or do you want to say sorry? Because if you apologize, me and the boys will let you go. So what's it going to be?"

"I'm sorry," says Tel.

My heart rate drops a little. They're going to let him go.

"See? That wasn't so hard, was it?" says Colt.

"I'm sorry you're such a MORON," says Tel.

Oh no.

Colt stands up and claps me on the shoulder. "All right," he says. "Finn. You're the latest member of our gang."

I recoil a little. They called Dad and Uncle Shane's thing a "gang", and hearing myself described as being in one makes me feel sick. I'm not sure why.

"Now it's time for you to prove yourself."

"What do you mean?" I say.

"You want him to spell it out for you?" asks Jay, getting in my face. "Hit him!"

"Yeah," says Dylan. "I'm jealous. I've been itching to have a dig myself."

Tel looks at me for the first time. There's an expression on his face, like he's trying to tell me something. We lock eyes. There's something there. Something familiar. A flash in my brain. It's night-time. I'm standing by the garages. Oh. *Oh.*

"No," I say.

"You what?" says Colt, shoving me.

Jay and Dylan round on me. "You soft or something?" says Jay.

"I'm not doing it," I say, trying to keep the tremor out of my voice. "It's not right. You need to let him go."

Dylan shoves me hard and I trip over a tree stump and land on my bum.

"Maybe we should tie *him* up as well," says Jay.

"Good idea," says Colt, rubbing his hands together.

I jump up and try to run, but I'm yanked back by someone grabbing my hood. Dylan sits on me and pins my arms down. I struggle to get free, but he's too heavy. I yell, but Jay kneels next to me, and covers my mouth with his hand. I'm trapped. This would never have happened back home. They would never have done this to a Butcher. But that was only because of Dad. These kids have no idea who he is. Who he was. I spent my whole life in a bubble and now it's been popped.

The weight is lifted off me. Through the corner of my eye, I see Jay go flying, then Dylan. Tel is up and advancing on them. They're running away. They're running away!

I scramble to my feet and dust myself down. "Thanks," I say.

Tel rolls his eyes. "Well, right back at you. If you didn't have your little attack of conscience there, I wouldn't have been able to wriggle out." He rubs his wrist. It looks sore. "I'm Tel, and you are?"

"Finn," I say.

Tel raises his eyebrows. "Short for Phineas?"

"No," I say. "It's not short for anything. It's just Finn. Anyway, what's their problem? Why are they after you all the time?"

"Because they think they run this place," says Tel. "Mini Ronnies. Anyone they see as weaker than them is always going to be victimized. They won't win, though. They won't win."

Well, I think they've figured out by now he's definitely not weaker than them. We stand quietly for a few seconds. Tel seems to be listening for any sign of them returning.

"Where did you learn to fight like that?" I ask him. I've seen fights at school before, but they were always just a bit of shoving and maybe some rolling around on the floor. He actually fights.

"The community centre," says Tel. "Jiu-jitsu."

We stand and listen for a moment. It doesn't look like they're coming back.

"You should watch yourself," says Tel. "They're going to be after you now, too."

"I know," I say. "Maybe I should learn jiu-jitsu, too."

Tel chuckles. "Maybe you should. Anyway, as much as this has been a pleasure, I should probably make haste."

"Wait."

Tel stops and turns around. He looks alert, like every muscle in his body is ready to respond to a threat that could come from anywhere.

"Yes?"

I smile. "You're Star Kid, aren't you?"

His mouth drops open a little, but then he seems to catch himself and the same neutral expression falls across his face.

"I haven't the faintest idea what you're talking about."

I have no doubt it's him. I can tell by the way he moves. Sure, the voice is different, but that Star Kid growl was obviously put on.

"You found my sister the other night," I say. "Thank you."

Tel runs his tongue along his lips and narrows his eyes at me. "So am I right in thinking that the only reason you didn't hit me was because you thought I was some superhero that saved your sister?"

"No," I say. "I don't hit anyone who's done nothing to me. Actually, I've never hit anyone." What I don't say is it's because I've never needed to. "But I know you did a good thing for my family, and I really appreciate it."

Tel blinks hard. The threat of a smile dances across his mouth. "I'll see you around, Phineas," he says.

CHAPTER 10

Weekends on the estate are pretty much the same as weekdays: boring. Mum has her first shift at Gino's today, so it's just me, Millie and Dad in the flat. Dad sits in front of the TV all day, his face unchanging. At least in the old days he would actually do stuff with us when he was home on weekends, like taking us out for ice creams, paid for by notes he peeled off big wodges of cash from his pocket.

Dad keeps asking why I'm not going out. I say I don't feel well. I'm not about to tell him I've got a gang – yes, an actual gang – after me. We've been here less than a week and I'm already a marked man. Like father, like son. I'm beginning to think Colt is even worse than Uncle Shane. I eye the baseball bat Dad keeps next to his chair.

I'm so bored that I agree to play "Santa's House" with Millie. Santa's House is a simple game. Millie controls the Santa Claus toy Star Kid gave her, while I bring her other toys, one by one, and she decides whether they've been good or bad.

"George Pig!" Santa squeaks. "You have been a naughty boy! You are getting no presents!"

Millie stares at me like I'm supposed to be doing something. I wobble George backwards and forwards a little. "Oh no," I say.

Millie growls and snatches George off me. "You're doing it wrong, Damian. George always cries. Watch." She shakes George and makes a "wahhh, wahhh" noise.

So, yeah, it's an annoying game, but what else am I supposed to do? Sit with Dad and the Wall Bears and watch some old film and constantly get asked why I'm not going out?

When Mum comes home, Dad doesn't move. He doesn't even acknowledge her. Millie more than makes up for it, though, running at her, climbing her like a tree and peppering her face with kisses.

"I missed you, Mummy. I missed you, I missed you. Ooh, you smell like cakes."

"How was it?" I ask.

I notice Dad shoot a sharp look at me but pretend I don't.

"Great," says Mum. "It went really well."

Dad lets out a single "Ha" and turns up the TV. I see Mum's eyes slide over to him, then back to me. She mouths "It was really great" so Dad can't hear.

The rest of the day passes in a miserable fog. Dad is incredible like that. He can make a room feel like a birthday party or a funeral purely based on his mood. He radiates outwards, touching everything around him.

After silently eating dinner, Dad announces he's going out. Mum asks him where, but he just says "out" and leaves. The second the door closes, it's like sun poking through the clouds. We can smile again. Millie can play in the lounge and be as loud as she likes. Mum sends me down to the shop to buy Cherry Zingas and popcorn and we all sit together on the sofa and watch *Frozen* for the gazillionth time. Even though it's Millie's favourite and officially I don't actually like it, it's still great.

Now, I'm lying in bed. Millie is fast asleep in her bed just across from me while her blue unicorn night light casts a shadow across the wall. I heard

Dad come in about an hour ago. Then low voices in the kitchen. They weren't raised or angry, so I had to take that as a positive.

I'm trying to get to sleep, but it's hard here. Not only is my mattress lumpy, but my brain often doesn't want to play ball. I'll lie there worrying about when I have to eventually go to that school, or when Colt is going to catch me, or Dad's next bad mood. Writing them down doesn't work as well as it used to. Where's Marian the social worker when I need her? I need something bigger than a Worry Book. The only thing that works is if I close my eyes and imagine I'm back home. I'm hanging out with Freddie and Conor and Will. There's always money and I'm free to go wherever I like. I'm not penned in by dual carriageways.

Tap, tap, tap.

I sit up in bed. What was that? I look over at Millie, bathed in blue light, but she's still sound asleep. I must have imagined it. Maybe I was drifting to sleep and I started dreaming early, or something. I lie back down.

Tap, tap, tap.

That was real. Someone or something is tapping on our bedroom window, from the landing outside.

It's Colt. It has to be. I tiptoe-run into the lounge and scoop up Dad's bat.

Tap, tap, tap.

There it is again, almost as loud as my heartbeat rushing in my ears. I grip the edge of the curtain. *Three ... two ... one.*

No one there. Just the dark landing. What if it's a ghost? A dark shape steps out of the shadows and I shriek. It's all dressed in black. When it steps forward, I see the stars on its chest.

Right. It's him.

I glance at Millie, but she still hasn't stirred. Once she's asleep, she's asleep. I open the window.

"Have you lost your mind?" I whisper-shout.

"What makes you say that?" says Star Kid in that gruff voice.

"You're standing outside my bedroom window at night dressed like ... like *that.*"

"We need to talk," says Star Kid.

"But it's nearly eleven o'clock!"

"I am a creature of the night," Star Kid fires back. "Now, are you coming out or what?"

"Obviously not," I say.

I go to close the window, but Star Kid stops it with one hand. Man, he's strong.

"It's important," he says.

I sigh. I did say I appreciated what he did for Millie. Maybe I should hear him out. "Hold on a sec, let me get changed." I draw the curtains again and, as quietly as I can, change into a pair of jeans, a T-shirt and a hoodie. After thinking about it for a second, I put the bat back in the lounge, then climb out of the window, leaving it a little open at the bottom so I can get back in.

"Come on," says Star Kid. "We'll find somewhere more secluded."

We walk down the stairs, across the car park and along the street until we arrive at the tallest block on the estate: Primrose House. Star Kid leads me inside and jabs the lift button for floor eight – the top floor.

It's kind of awkward inside. How are you supposed to make small talk with someone in a superhero costume? Under the lift lights, I can see it's actually pretty good, for an amateur effort. It's not the kind of thing you'd buy for a fancy-dress party; it's custom-made, like one of those cosplayers you see on Instagram.

The lift stops and Star Kid leads me past some flats and up a flight of stairs, then he opens a door and we're on the roof, overlooking Ampleforth. In the distance, past the dual carriageway, lights from houses beyond the estate twinkle like stars.

"Do you have all your conversations up here?" I ask him.

"No," he says. "I just needed to come somewhere I'm sure we won't be disturbed."

I step close to the edge and look down at the street lights below. My stomach twists. It's a long way down.

Star Kid stares at me, his eyes shining in the dark. His lips tighten into a thin line. He looks like he wants to say something.

"So, are you going to come out with it, or not?" I say. "If my sister wakes up and I'm not there, she's going to freak."

Star Kid's mouth loosens and he takes a deep breath. Then, he reaches up and peels off his mask. It's Tel. I mean, who else is it going to be?

"Oh, wow," I say. "This is the most shocking thing I've ever seen in my life."

"Very funny, Phineas," he says in his normal voice. "So how did you know?"

"That day with Colt and the others. I could tell from your" – I wave my hand up and down, not knowing the right way to phrase it – "body."

Tel laughs. "That distinctive, is it?"

I think this is the first time I've seen him smile properly. It's weird. It changes his whole face. I can see that, even in the dark. It makes his eyes twinkle. As far as smiles go, it's a good one. Wait a second, how long have I been staring at him?

"Oh. I, uh, didn't mean it like that," I blurt. "It was just how you fought them off. It was … superhero … y."

Tel cocks his head to one side, hands on hips, that smile still on his face. It doesn't look like he's going to say anything and I can't help but keep talking to fill the silence.

"So, is that why you're doing this Star Kid thing? Protect yourself from bullies?"

Tel drops his hand, then seems to check his fingernails even though he's wearing gloves. "My reasons are many and varied, Phineas."

It doesn't look like he's going to tell me what they are, though. I see a shadow, maybe a bat, skitter through the lamplight below then disappear into darkness.

"Is this the important thing that couldn't wait, then?" I ask. "You wanted to tell me what a genius I am for figuring out your big secret?"

Tel rolls his eyes. "Hardly. I just wanted to clear the air. Remove any confusion from the situation. I thought it only fair. Especially when you helped me back there. Plus..." He frowns and shakes his head. "Forget it, it's stupid."

"No, what?"

He turns his back on me. "I said forget it."

I put my hand on his shoulder and turn him around. "Come on," I say.

Tel looks at the ground. He seems a little shy about something. "When I started doing, well, *this*, a few months ago, I didn't envisage doing it alone."

"What do you mean?" I say. "And it's too late at night for you to be using words like 'envisage'."

Tel narrows his eyes at me. "My aim has always been to be part of a team. An ensemble, if you will. You know, like the Avengers?"

I nod. I've seen the movies.

"And I was wondering if..." He sighs. "I was wondering if you'd consider joining my aforementioned ensemble."

I laugh, but Tel looks completely serious. "Me?" I say.

Tel nods.

"But you don't know me!" I say. "And besides, I can't fight or anything like that. You saw what happened the other day – my bum is still bruised."

"That is immaterial," says Tel. "The reason I thought of you is because you know right from wrong. You have a conscience."

"And no one else around here has a conscience?"

"Of course they do. But kids our age? They don't want to be seen to have one. It's not cool or something, I don't know."

"So you're saying I'm not cool?"

"Exactly!" Tel smiles that dazzling, twinkling smile again. "And that's why you're the perfect candidate! Believe me, I've been searching high and low for the next member of my team and come away with diddly zero. Then, one day, you show up out of nowhere!"

"I don't know," I say. "I mean, for one thing, I don't really know anything about superheroes."

"You would be spectacular!" says Tel. "Besides, I have comics you can borrow for inspiration. It might take a little time to figure out what you're good at, but once you do, you're away."

"Can I let you know?" I say, hoping that will get me away from him.

"Yes." Tel grips my shoulders. "Sleep on it, Phineas. Let me know tomorrow."

I leave him on the roof, make my way home, and climb back in through the window. Millie is still asleep. It's all I can do not to laugh out loud. Me as a superhero? Yeah, right.

CHAPTER 11

After breakfast, Mum gives me some money and sends me down to the shop to get some bits for lunch later. She always does a roast on Sundays, and I think she wants to make the first one in our new flat extra special. It would have to be the roast of the century to make up for the extreme crumminess of our new surroundings, but let's give it a chance.

I step outside our front door when WHAM. I walk straight into Tel.

"Have you been hanging around on the landing all night?" I whisper-shout.

"Clearly not," he says. "I mean, I'm not in my costume."

"Why didn't you just knock on the door?" I ask, wondering when my heart rate is going to return to normal.

Tel shrugs. "I'm not much of a door-knocker. So, have you considered my proposition?"

I look at my watch. "It's not even ten o'clock!"

"Right," says Tel. "So you've had eleven hours. That's plenty of time."

I troop past Tel and he follows me down the stairs.

"What do you actually do, anyway?" I ask him. "Just walk around at night?"

"I'm aiming to make the estate a better, safer place," says Tel. "And I'm doing pretty well. I mean, I found your sister, didn't I?"

"Great," I say, as we cross the car park. "So why do you need me?"

"Because, Phineas, with two of us, we can do twice as much," says Tel. "Don't make me explain basic maths to you."

I can't help but smile. I like Tel. He's nothing like my old friends. He's clever and he's funny and he obviously isn't bothered about what people think of him. I'd like to hang out with him, not Star Kid.

When we reach the shops, he grabs my arm. "Look around you," he says.

I do as he tells me, but I don't know what I'm supposed to be looking at. I mean, it's a dump.

"This estate is full of kind, generous people," says Tel. "We're not rich, but we always help each other out. Who wouldn't want to protect that from bad guys?" He points at the community centre. There's a woman outside in a flowery cardigan, whistling cheerfully as she loads bags of food into a trolley. "See that lady? That's Pat. She runs the food bank."

"What's a food bank?"

Tel side-eyes me. "Where did you move here from, anyway? Monte Carlo?"

"No," I say, feeling my stress levels rising at the thought of being questioned about where I came from. "I just don't know what a food bank is, that's all."

"Lucky you," he says. "Hey, why don't we hear it straight from the horse's mouth? Greetings, Pat!"

Tel walks over to Pat and I follow. When she sees him, she smiles. "Hello, Tel! Still cracking those books, are you?"

"Certainly," he says. "The philosophy one I've got now is excellent."

Pat laughs. "Well, you know where the library is

when you want another one." She turns her attention to me. She has rosy cheeks and kind, twinkly eyes. "I haven't seen you before."

"This is Phineas," says Tel. "He's new around here."

Pat clicks her finger. "Hold on, wasn't it your sister who went missing the other night?"

I nod, kind of embarrassed. "And it's Finn, not Phineas."

"Oh, I was so worried," says Pat. "Me and my husband, Stan, went all over the place looking for her. Not that he was much use. He left his bifocals at home and thought a Great Dane was your sister."

"I was just telling PHINEAS about the food bank, and he said he didn't know what they were for," says Tel.

Pat nods. "Well, to be honest, it's a shame we have to have them in the first place. But we can only live in the world we're given, you know what I mean, my love?"

"Yeah," I say, thinking about my tiny bedroom in our tiny flat.

"So the food bank runs entirely on donations," says Pat, "and anyone who's struggling to afford to feed their family can come down and we'll help them."

"Really?" I say. "People can just come down and get free food?"

Pat frowns. "I wouldn't put it like that, my love. These people have often fallen on hard times. We're the only thing keeping them from going hungry. Like I say, in a perfect world, we wouldn't be needed."

Tel waggles his eyebrows at me. Well, consider me educated.

"That must be a cool job," I say to Pat.

"Oh, it's not a job." She loads another bag into her trolley. "No one pays me to do this."

"Seriously?" I blurt out. "So you do it for nothing?"

"No money, if that's what you mean," says Pat. "But what is money compared to the satisfaction you get from helping someone in need? To lightening their load just a little bit?"

What she's saying makes sense, it really does. It just goes against anything Dad ever taught me. "If they want money they should get jobs, like the rest of us," he'd always say, even though he never had a job. Not a normal one, anyway.

Whenever we walked past a homeless person back home, he'd hurry by.

"Well, I think that's told him!" says Tel. "We'll see you soon!"

88

As we walk away, Tel jabs my arm. "See?" he says. "We're a close community here, but we know that no one from outside is coming to help us, so we all do our bit to pitch in. Some of us feed the hungry, some of us stalk the night in search of crime. Potayto, potahto."

I sigh. "Yeah, but I've only just got here."

"All the more reason to get started now," says Tel. "Besides, it can't have escaped your attention how other people helped your family in their time of need, even though you had, as you put it, just got here?"

He's got me there. Which is really annoying.

"OK, fine," I say. "But couldn't I do something easier, like, I don't know, picking litter or whatever?"

"If you like," says Tel. "Or maybe we incorporate that into your superhero identity: Garbage Boy!"

I groan. "All right, I see you aren't going to let this go," I say. "But even if I were to agree to your wacky scheme, WHICH I WON'T, I don't have a costume or anything."

Tel gently pats my cheek. "Don't you worry your pretty little face about that. I will sort you out in no time."

I turn towards the shop. Mum is going to be wondering where I am.

"Come on," says Tel. "Haven't you always wanted to be a hero?"

Now, that makes me stop and think. Do I want to be a hero? Sure, people cheering you on while you save the world seems fun, but it's kind of a lot of work. Still, maybe it *could* be fun? Something to do at least?

I think he can tell my brain is whirring, because he grabs my arm and says,

"Let me show you what costumes I have."

CHAPTER 12

We're in Tel's flat on the third floor of Primrose House. He followed me to the shop, and then home with the stuff. I had no way out.

No one is home. He tells me it's just him and his mum now his older brother has gone off to university. "He's studying to be an astrophysicist and is currently on a work placement in Switzerland. How am I supposed to compete with that?" He doesn't mention anything about his dad, so I guess he's out of the picture in some way. I would ask, but it feels kind of nosy.

Tel escorts me to his bedroom. His room is about the same size as mine, but it's nicer. Like, it's obviously been decorated at some point in the last twenty years and it's neat, and more importantly, he has it to himself.

At the far end, by the window, is a desk with a sewing machine on it. Next to it stands a mannequin with a tight blue outfit pinned on.

"So what do you think?" says Tel, waving an arm around the room.

"Not exactly the Batcave," I say. "Does your mum know about the whole ... superhero thing?"

He shakes his head. "She just thinks I'm really into fashion. OK, let's get down to brass tacks, Phineas."

Tel kneels on the floor and pulls a big storage box out from under his bed. It's stuffed with superhero costumes of every colour you could imagine.

"What are these, like, prototypes?" I ask him, vaguely remembering something similar in one of those *Iron Man* movies.

"No," says Tel, "I made all of these for my future team of superheroes. Now, how about this one?" He pulls out a bright green costume with spindly legs sticking out of the side. "The Grasshopper!"

I raise my eyebrows. "The Grasshopper?"

"Well, all the best creepy-crawlies are taken," he says, counting off on his fingers. "Ant-Man, Wasp,

Bumblebee, Spider-Man. It doesn't leave us with much."

"I'm not being the Grasshopper," I say.

Tel rolls his eyes. He does that a lot. "Fine. You're such a fussbudget. Right, how about this?" He pulls out a red, white and green striped costume and a pair of boots with curled-up toes.

"What the blue hell is that?" I say.

Tel lowers his voice and whispers dramatically, "The Elf of Justice."

"The Nope of Nopestice."

Tel looks slightly offended, but I can tell he's not going to give up.

"Look," I say. "If I'm going to do this – and that is a very big *if* – I don't want to look like an idiot. Especially next to you, all dark and brooding."

Tel shakes his head, smiling. "But it's the classic formula. It's not Batman and Batman Two, is it? It's Batman and Robin. It's the contrast that makes it pop."

"What, so I'm Robin? I'm not sure about that."

"How about this one?" Tel scoops up a yellow costume and jumps to his feet, displaying it with a proud grin on his face. On the chest, there are thin, jagged orange lines. It's by far the least embarrassing one he's shown me.

"Not bad," I say. "What is it called?"

"Sunbeam," says Tel.

"You're joking, right?"

Tel sends me into the bathroom to try it on. It's kind of stiff. Heavier than I was expecting, too. There's a zip on the back and I can't get it all the way up. I resist the temptation to look in the mirror until I have the mask on. When I pull it down over my head, it feels weird. Kind of baggy. The eyeholes move around a bit. I look in the mirror. Wow. I look like a little kid trying on his dad's superhero costume. There's a knock at the door.

"Come on, then," says Tel. "Let's see Sunbeam."

I unlock the door and open it. "Not Sunbeam. And I look ridiculous."

Tel looks like he's stifling a laugh. "It's nothing a few adjustments won't fix."

"A lot of adjustments!" I lift my arm and wobble the loose flappy bit underneath. "Look at me, I've got bingo wings!"

At this, Tel dissolves into fits of laughter and I have to stand there and wait for him to stop.

"I'm sorry," he says, wiping his eyes. "It's just when I thought about my first team member, I imagined them to be" – he stops and moves his

hands around, like he's juggling invisible balls –
"more substantial."

"Well, I'm sorry to disappoint you."

Tel waves me off. "Oh, don't be silly, you're wonderful just as you are. A unique, spectacular snowflake."

He steps closer and pinches the excess material. He frowns in concentration while his lips move soundlessly. When he's done, he stands back and looks at me. "OK, slip that back off and bring it to the lab."

"The lab?"

"My bedroom," he says.

Five minutes later, I'm watching Tel hunched over his sewing machine with that same expression of concentration on his face.

"So what's the school like?" I ask, trying to imagine how someone like him fits in.

"Like the seventh circle of hell, why do you ask?" he replies, pressing down on the pedal that makes the machine go.

"Just curious," I say. "So you don't have any friends at all?"

"One of the lunch servers is pretty friendly."

"No girls you like?"

Tel laughs. "Girls aren't really my thing, Phineas. Not like that anyway."

"Oh," I say.

He looks at me for the first time in ages, an eyebrow raised. "You're OK with that?"

"Um, yeah," I say. I mean, I am. It's just I don't think I've ever met a boy that likes boys before. And Dad often lets me know what he thinks of people like that.

"Well, that's a relief," says Tel, the machine buzzing again. "Boys usually think that I want nothing more than to passionately kiss them at the drop of a hat. I'm like, I do have standards, you know."

"So how did you get into this?" I ask him, wanting to change the subject, but not knowing why.

"Through my brother," says Tel, clamping a couple of pins between his teeth. "He's a big cosplayer. That's the worst thing about him being away at uni. I have no one to go to Comic Con with any more. Anyway, one night I had a brainwave: why don't I create my own costumes? I've still got the designs in that drawer. Have a look, if you like."

I open the drawer and pull out a thick black book. Every page is filled with these amazing, detailed sketches. I flip through and watch as the Star Kid costume evolves from a line drawing into a full colour design. Then there are all the others; the Grasshopper, the Elf of Justice, Sunbeam.

"You're a genius," I say.

"Oh, stop, I am not," says Tel over the buzz of the sewing machine. "I'm just really, really talented. And handsome. Right." He releases the needle on the machine and pulls the costume off. "Try that on for size, big boy."

This time, it fits much better. I look at myself in the mirror, and I kind of look good. No bingo wings, anyway. Tel knocks on the door and I let him in. He grins that electric grin. "Now that's what I'm talking about," he says. "All we need to do now is fit your mask."

He comes over and carefully pulls the mask down over my head. This time it fits perfectly. As well as the eye holes, there is a gap for my mouth and a small one for the bottom of my nose. Tel does one of those chef's kiss things. "Wow. Sunbeam. It's like you've sashayed off the pages of my design book."

I look at myself in the mirror again and, for a second, I'm knocked off-balance. It's like there's a different person staring back. It sounds stupid when I say it in my head, but I feel powerful, older, stronger.

"Wow," I whisper. "I'm a superhero."

Tel grips my shoulders and gives them a firm squeeze. "Yes, you are, Phineas. Yes, you are."

CHAPTER 13

This suit was not meant to be slept in. I'm lying under my covers in full Sunbeam costume, minus the mask, waiting for Tel to call. I'm trying to read one of the comics he gave me by the light of my phone.

"It's a selection from both of the big boys," he had said, as he pressed the stack of about fifteen comics into my hands. "It will give you a grounding in all things superhero."

I've never read a comic before and I don't know why, because they're really fun. It's all explosions and bad guys getting kicked in the face. Right now, though, I'm too nervous to concentrate.

I had to wait until Millie fell asleep before I put on the costume. That's when I realized how noisy it was. Every creak of the rubber made her stir. At one point, I heard footsteps going past our door. How would I explain myself if Mum or Dad walked in? Mum, I could probably swing it, but Dad? I dread to think what he'd do.

Thankfully, I avoided detection, and when the *tap, tap, tap* at the bedroom window comes, I'm ready to go. I stand up, slip on my mask and climb out of the window.

"You look fierce," says Star Kid.

I think about it for a second. "Is that a good thing?"

"Definitely. Let's go."

It's eleven o'clock. I'd normally be asleep at this time, but I'm wide awake, buzzing with excitement. I am a real-life superhero.

"CHUFFIN' NORA!" An old man on his way home from the pub yells as we leave Ambrose Court. "WHAT HAVE YOU TWO COME AS?"

"I am Star Kid!" says Tel, all gravelly.

"And I'm…" I hesitate for a second. "Sunbeam." I still haven't come up with anything better.

The old man chuckles and shakes his head. "Best of luck to you," he says, then continues his amble up the dark street.

"OK." Star Kid turns to me. "We need to talk about your voice."

"What's wrong with my voice?"

"Nothing," says Star Kid. "It's beautiful, mellifluous, like a majestic starling. It's just, I can't have you walking around sounding like that."

"Sounding like what?" I say, getting even more self-conscious.

"Listen to me," he replies. "I didn't just speak to that gentleman in this voice, did I? This is not the voice of a superhero."

Oh, yeah. He uses this kind of deep, gruff voice when he's Star Kid.

"It helps protect my identity," he goes on. "Because if someone I know hears me talking like this, they're going to be like, 'Hang on, isn't that Tel?'"

"OK, I get your point," I say. "So what voice am I supposed to do?"

"That's up to you," says Star Kid. "Don't overthink it. Just let your soul sing."

I take a deep breath and try to do as he says. "Hello," I say, in this voice that for some reason sounds like a parrot. "I'm Sunbeam."

Star Kid splutters and then recovers his composure.

"Hey!" I say. "I'm trying my best!"

"I know you are," says Star Kid. "And I love you for that. Look, have another go, just maybe take it down an octave or two."

I blink hard and take another breath. "I'M SUNBEAM," I growl. This time, I go too deep and I sound like I'm about to hock up a greeny.

Star Kid tilts his head, his hand on his hips. "Huh. Well, it's an improvement. Look, there's nothing wrong with being a silent superhero. Something to think about, maybe. The Ampleforth Avengers will need heroes of all kinds."

"Ampleforth Avengers?" I say. "Not very original, is it?"

"Well, can you think of a better name?"

I search my brain for something. The Ampleforth Acrobats? No, that doesn't work. The Ampleforth Architects? That's ridiculous. The Ampleforth Arsonists? That's … just no.

"Well, I consider my point proven," says Star Kid.

We head to the roof of Primrose House and look out over the estate. Not much seems to be happening from what I can make out in the dark. A couple of people slowly walking up the cycle path, a man scrolling on his phone outside his house. In the distance, a police car speeds up the dual carriageway with its lights flashing, but it's heading away from us.

"So why are superheroes even needed?" I ask Star Kid. "I mean, you've got police, haven't you?"

Star Kid chuckles. "I guess. But they can't do everything. There's a lot of things that have happened here that have gone unresolved. A lot of things."

Even though he's under his Star Kid mask, I sense Tel's mood getting darker. His eyelids droop, his mouth tightens.

"Everything all right?"

He shakes his head quickly. "Yes, fine. Enough about that. I feel like we need to learn more about Sunbeam. Or at least, the man behind the lovely yellow cowl. Like, where did you come from?"

"My mum's tummy," I say. "Hey, is that a fox down there?"

He swats my arm. "Come on. You just showed up on the estate as if from nowhere. I don't really know anything about you."

I look out at the horizon, where the red lights on the TV mast seem to hover in the darkness like seven red UFOs in perfect formation. I could tell him. Could tell him everything. But how do I know if I can trust him? If he goes and tells someone, they'll tell someone, and then they'll tell someone, and eventually everyone will know. Like Colt said, word travels fast on the estate. And then we'll be in trouble. Deep trouble.

"I'm from Atherworth," I say.

"Shut up!" says Star Kid. "My cousins live there! What school did you go to?"

Oh, bum. Bum, bum, bum. The programme people told me the name of the school in Atherworth and I'm completely drawing a blank. What kind of idiot can't remember the name of their own school?

"You know," I say. "The, um, the big one."

Star Kid is looking at me now: closely and steadily, his eyes focused. "The big one, eh?" he says, quietly. "Bishop Blaize School?"

I clap. "That's the one. Bishop Blaize."

Star Kid nods, his bottom lip jutting out. "Interesting." Then something distracts him. I don't know what it is, but I am eternally grateful to it.

"See those gentlemen down there?" He points at two shadows moving across the car park. "I've seen them loitering outside the community centre every night this week."

"Right," I say. "And what are they doing?"

"Haven't the foggiest," he says. "But I'm worried they're planning something."

"Like what?" I say.

Star Kid narrows his eyes, following them as they move towards the community centre. "Robbery? Vandalism? Let's go down and get a closer look."

We take the lift down and head towards the community centre. My stomach starts to flutter. This is it. This is really it. I can't figure out whether I'm more worried about getting hurt or looking stupid.

"We need to be as quiet as we can," says Star Kid. "If they hear us coming, they might get spooked."

"We're not going to attack them, are we?" I say, my stomach flutters upgrading to full blown spasms of panic.

"No, we're going to stake them out," says Star Kid. "Hide in the shadows and see if we can parse their intentions."

We go the long way around the community centre and creep under the canopy around the side. I see two men standing outside Gino's. They're older than I was expecting, even older than my mum and dad. They're deep in conversation, but are so quiet I can't make out any words.

"Do you recognize them?" I whisper to Star Kid.

"I've seen one of them around," he whispers back. "The fellow in the black jacket. Don't know who he is, though."

I peer through the gloom for a closer look. "He doesn't exactly look like a criminal. He just looks like some bloke."

"What were you expecting, a mask and a stripy jumper?" asks Star Kid. "Not all criminals look like criminals. Trust me."

I swallow hard and try to ignore the discomfort building in my brain. The other man is smoking a cigarette and keeps shifting from foot to foot. I see what Tel means now. They are acting kind of weird.

"I want to get a little closer," says Star Kid. "See if we can hear what they're saying."

We creep forward, centimetre by centimetre, making sure to stay in the shadows. I try to listen, but it's still a low murmur.

"Can I help you?" says the bloke in the black jacket.

"Blend in," Star Kid breathes. "Become the darkness."

"I can see you there," says the other bloke. "You're dressed in bright yellow."

I shoot Tel a glance. Become the darkness? You might as well ask me to become a sausage roll. Star Kid growls under his breath and steps into the lamplight.

"What's going on?" asks Black Jacket, laughing a little. "Are we being mugged?"

"I'm Star Kid," he says, in that gruff voice.

"And I'm the Incredible Hulk, pleased to meet you," Black Jacket shoots back.

"We were just wondering what you two were up to this evening," says Star Kid. I stand behind him and try to look menacing, even though I'm pretty sure I'm pulling the same face I do when I'm trying to hold in a fart.

The smoking guy laughs. "Just having a chat. Who are you supposed to be, anyway?"

"We've already told you that," says Star Kid. "Now you tell us why you've been here every night this week."

The man waves his hands around. "We just enjoy the ambience," he says. "Beautiful scenery. Now, if you don't mind…"

"I've seen you before," says Star Kid, refusing to move. "You work for Ronnie, don't you?"

The man stops smiling. "I don't know what you're talking about."

Star Kid nods, hands on hips. "Of course you don't."

We head across the car park after it becomes clear that the blokes aren't going to give up their reason for hanging around the precinct.

"Something's not right," says Star Kid.

"Too right, something's not right!" I snap back at him. "I'm supposed to stalk the night, blending in with the shadows, and I'm walking around dressed like a giant highlighter pen."

Star Kid tuts. "All right, fine, I'll sort that out."

"Don't bother," I say. "I think that's it for me."

"What are you talking about?"

"Well, it didn't exactly go well, did it?" I say. "I felt like a right idiot."

"Don't do anything rash, Sunbeam," says Star Kid. "There are always teething problems when you first start out."

"I gave it a try. And I didn't like it."

We arrive outside my block.

"I'll give you the outfit back tomorrow."

Star Kid looks crestfallen, but what am I supposed to do? I can't carry on doing this. I climb back in through the window, carefully peel off the costume and shove it under my bed. Millie is sleeping soundly now. Best to just stick to normal life, eh?

CHAPTER 14

Normal life sucks.

Dad came home from work in a stinking mood. He'd left in one, too, after he'd barged into our room and found my stack of comics. He was all "Since when are you into this garbage?" and "These are for kids. I thought you were supposed to be growing up?" It was the same kind of disappointed talk he gave me when I dropped out of the school football team.

Now, though, it's gone to another level. He slams the door so hard, a framed photo falls off the wall and smashes.

"Was that really necessary?" asks Mum.

Dad doesn't answer, just sits in his hard chair. But then he gets up again and points at Mum as she tries to clean up the mess.

"This is all your fault!" he yells.

Millie scooches closer to me on the sofa and starts sucking her thumb.

"What are you talking about?" says Mum.

"I would have done the time," he says. "I would have had my honour and dignity at least. I should never have listened to you."

Mum stands upright and fidgets with her hands, nervously. I feel bad because she was in a great mood before Dad came home. Everyone was. Mum had been at work at Gino's, Millie had been to the day care and was telling us all about the new friends she'd made, and I'd at least not had a horrible day. I'd stayed at home, and so avoided Colt, so that's something. I did kind of miss Tel, but I tried not to think about it too much. But now, here was Dad, yet again, like a storm cloud over a picnic.

"Please try and calm down, love," said Mum, her voice soft. "It's all very well having dignity and honour, but what good is that when you're in prison and your family is homeless? They would have taken the house; you know they would, sweetheart. Besides, if you hadn't … done what you did, someone else would. Look, what's the matter? Has something happened?"

Dad paces back and forth, running his hands through his hair. "It's that boss," he says. "I got sick of him."

"What did you do?" says Mum, her voice wobbling a little.

Dad stops pacing. "Nothing," he says. "I just got sick of him, that's all."

He sits down and this time it looks like he isn't moving. He glares hard at something on the floor: one of Tel's comics. I should have moved that before he got back. He stays silent, though.

I glance over at Mum and I can tell we're thinking the same thing. There's something he's not telling us.

Worry Book

What has he done now?

CHAPTER 15

Tap, tap, tap.

I groan and press my pillow over my face.

Tap, tap, tap.

"Go away," I say, my words muffled by the pillow.

Tap, tap, tap.

I jump out of bed and throw open the window.

"Can't you take no for an answer?"

But it's not Star Kid. Not exactly. It's Tel, in his normal clothes. He's carrying a holdall.

"Hear me out," he says.

"I told you I'm finished," I say, but seeing him standing here now, looking all superheroey even without the costume, I wonder if I really mean it.

"Please." He puts the bag down and opens the zip, then reaches in and pulls out a costume. This one is like his Star Kid costume, but instead of stars, there are crescent moons. I don't want to admit it, but it looks amazing.

"What do you think?" he says with a shy smile.

"Very nice," I say. "It will look good on whoever decides to join your team."

"But it's custom made for you," he says. "It wouldn't fit anyone else."

Millie stirs and moans a little in her sleep. "Well, that's bad luck," I whisper. "Because I'm not putting it on."

"Oh, come on, Phineas," says Tel. "I worked on this for twenty-four hours with no break. I'm so tired I can hardly see straight. The least you can do is try it on."

"Wrong," I say. "The least I can do is close the window and go to bed."

Tel shakes his head sadly. "I thought you were different, Phineas. I really did."

"You don't know the half of it," I mumble.

"I gave you a name," says Tel. "Moon Boy."

Star Kid and Moon Boy? It did sound better than Sunbeam. Looked better, too.

I think Tel can sense I'm thinking about it because he presses further. "You can't tell me you've never wanted a secret identity," he says.

I've already got one. What's one more, I suppose?

"Fine," I say. "I'll try it on, but that's it."

I take the costume from Tel and close the window behind me. I carefully open the bedroom door. Mum is in bed and Dad is watching TV in the lounge. It's two steps to the bathroom, but my heart is pounding like it's two miles. This isn't like the old house, where I knew the exact locations of the creaky floorboards. I have to quite literally tread carefully. If Dad catches me with this costume, what chance do I have of explaining myself?

I take one step. I'm glad he's watching something with loads of explosions in it. I take another step. I wait for another boom before pushing the door open and locking it behind me.

I could have just put it on in the bedroom, but I'd risk waking Millie, who was already stirring, and besides, we don't have a mirror in our room. I kind of want to see how it looks.

I turn on the tap to drown out the sounds of me putting on the suit. Tel's right. It does fit. Just as well as the Sunbeam suit did. Maybe better. I pull down the mask and look at myself in the mirror. Wow. I look cool. It's been ages since I've felt cool. This is different from Sunbeam. I don't feel like such a sidekick this time. I feel more like an equal. Maybe I *could* give it another go?

The door rattles. *No, no, no, no.*

"Is that you, Damian?" says Dad.

What can I do? It's not as if I can deny it. Also, it's FINN.

"Yep," I say.

"Can you hurry up? I need to go."

Stupid flat with its stupid lack of bathrooms.

"OK," I say, yanking my mask off. "Just give me a minute."

"What are you doing in there, anyway?" he says. "How come you're running so much water?"

"Just brushing my teeth!"

I pull the costume down, but it's tight and I'm sweating, and it makes a sound like a long, ripping fart.

"Brushing your teeth, eh?" chuckles Dad. "Make sure to spray some air freshener when you're done."

With the costume off and my pyjamas back on, I'm stuck. Where am I supposed to put it? There is nowhere to hide it. If I put it in the bath, Dad will see it. The cabinet above the sink is so tiny, it would barely hold the mask. I could shove it up my top and pretend I've put on a lot of weight recently.

That's an option. Oh, what am I saying? I'm done for. Unless…

The bathroom window can be opened wide enough for me to get it through. The only problem is, there isn't a landing that side, just a long drop into the yard of a ground floor flat. But what alternative is there?

I fold up the costume, then open the stiff bathroom window and post it through. I hope there's no one down there. Then I shut the window, turn off the tap and open the door.

"About time," Dad huffs as he rushes past me.

With the door safely locked behind me, I tiptoe-run back to my room and open the window. Tel looks confused.

"I thought you were trying the costume on."

I climb out of the window and jump on to the landing. "It's in someone's yard. Long story."

We run down the staircase and out of the main door. I look up at our flat and try to work out which yard it landed in. It must have been number twelve.

"Why would you throw it out of the window?" Tel cries.

"My dad nearly caught me and I panicked," I say.

"It's a costume, not beer," Tel snaps. "I swear to all

that is holy, if you have damaged this costume in any way, I will murder you to death."

Number twelve is all in darkness. All I have to do is go in the front bit, get the costume and get out. Easy. I carefully open the gate. The yard is covered in boxes draped in fine, green nets. It looks like vegetables growing: beans and stuff like that. Yes! There's the costume, lying half draped over the fence. I quickly snatch it up and pass it over the gate to Tel.

"Well, it looks like it survived the fall unscathed," says Tel. "Now find the mask."

Oh no, I forgot about the mask. Where is it? I scan the floor for any sign, but I can't see it. If this had happened to Sunbeam, I'd have found it in a split second. Hold on a sec. What's that over by the front door? It's the mask! I run over and scoop it up.

WHOOMPH!

The door opens and a beast charges at me, growling, teeth bared. I scream and run for the gate, but the beast is faster and backs me against the fence. I try to open the gate, but it needs to come inwards and there's no room.

"Tel!" I squeak. "I'm going to die!"

Another shape appears in the doorway. "Lola! Lola! Come here!"

This beast is called Lola? Not Beelzebub?

Lola obediently runs back to her master, tail wagging. The shape from the doorway steps closer and looks at me.

"Finn? What are you doing in my yard?"

The lamplight illuminates the face of the shape.

"Oh," I say, relief washing over me. "Hello, Gino."

He folds his arms with a confused smile.

"Sorry about this," I say. "I, um, accidentally knocked, um, this out of the window."

Gino chuckles. "And what are you doing with that thing, robbing banks?"

I laugh, too, possibly a little too loud. "No, no, just going to a fancy-dress party."

Gino seems a little confused, but it looks like he's going to let it slide.

"Sorry about Lola," he says. "She's a good watch dog, but she's soft as gelato. Isn't that right, girl?" Gino kneels and starts fussing her, making her tail wag so hard, she almost snaps some bean poles. Now I can look at her when she's not chasing me, she seems quite nice. A German shepherd, by the looks of it.

"That's OK," I say. "And I'm sorry for disturbing you."

Gino waves me off. "Think nothing of it. When you need your mask, you need your mask."

"Thanks, Gino," I say. I turn to leave, then stop. "Actually, could you do me a favour?"

"What is it?" he asks, ruffling Lola's fur.

"Could you not mention any of this to my mum?"

Gino salutes. "Your secret is safe with me."

As we walk towards the front door, Tel clasps my shoulder. "That was rather more eventful than I was expecting."

"You're telling me," I say. "I thought I was about to get my face chewed off."

We stop outside Ambrose Court and Tel holds the costume out to me. "So come on," he says. "Am I looking at the next Moon Boy or not?"

I look at the costume, then up at his face, that big smile full of excitement, and, behind him, the real moon and stars twinkle high above us.

"No," I say.

CHAPTER 16

To begin with, I thought having the flat to myself all day would be fun. I don't know why. It's not like it's Disney World. But by the time Mum was due to finish at Gino's, I was bored out of my skull. Turns out the Wall Bears aren't great company. Then, just as I thought I was about to have some *real* company, Mum called to say she was going to be working late and asked if I could pick up Millie from the day care. "Stop by the café on the way and I'll make it worth your while," she said.

So that's why I'm walking into Gino's now. Mum is behind the counter, laughing at something Gino is doing in the kitchen behind her. When she sees me, she stops.

"Oh, hello, Finn!"

"Is that your son, my love?" says an old lady, sitting at a table at the back. "Isn't he handsome?"

"He gets it all from me," says Mum, leaning over the counter and squeezing my cheek.

"Ha, ha," I say, flatly, my face turning red. "So what's this about you making something worth my while?"

Mum tuts theatrically and pulls a tenner out of her pocket. "It's for you and Millie to go and do something nice."

"Like what?" I say. "There's literally nothing to do here."

"I don't know," Mum says. "Maybe buy her a little toy from the shop, or something."

"Heyyy!" Gino comes out of the kitchen. "If it isn't the Lone Ranger!"

I have no idea what he's talking about, but I hope he's kept my secret.

"Sorry I'm keeping your mum late this afternoon," he says. "I've got to go into town to see the bank manager and someone needs to hold down the fort. Your mother here has proven to be a trustworthy and capable employee."

Mum chuckles. "So am I getting a pay rise, then?"

"Pay?" says Gino, raising an eyebrow. "I don't remember ever agreeing to pay you."

I leave them giggling at each other and pick Millie up from the day care. She is not happy about having to leave.

"But I was playing with Harvey!" she moans all the way out.

I see this Harvey at the fence shouting after her. His entire face is covered in what I hope is chocolate.

"Nice friend you've got there, Mils," I say.

Millie seems to only just clock that I'm not Mum and demands to know where she is.

"She's got to work late," I say. "But!" I get in there before she can moan. "She has given me some money to go and buy you a toy."

Millie's eyes go huge. "A toy?!"

"Yeah, but only from the corner shop, so try not to get your hopes up."

The shop is run by this bloke called Ali. He is a jolly, round man and everyone on the estate seems to love him. Nearly every time I've been in here, there have been people just popping in for a chat with him, often not even buying anything.

We find the little toy section, and even though I can see there's nothing but super-cheap rubbish, Millie is in hog heaven.

"It's so hard!" she says. "Do I want the doctor set or the toy fire engine?"

They're a pound each, so, much to her delight, I treat her to both. Plus, the obligatory bag of Cherry Zingas. It's a pretty hot day, too, so we stop by the freezer and pick up a couple of ice lollies. I'm reaching in for the very specific green one Millie wants when I sense a presence through the corner of my eye. It's weird when you can tell someone is staring at you without properly looking at them. I shoot my head up and see it's Colt, with his hood up. What am I going to do? I can't fight him off with a Calippo. Ali is in the stockroom behind us. I can hear him singing along with the radio.

"Who's that?" Millie asks. She leans on me, the way she always does when she's shy.

"Nobody," I say. "It's nobody."

Colt smiles, that chilling grin I last saw when Tel was tied to that pipe, but then Ali comes out of the stockroom with a box of crisps and the smile snaps away and Colt leaves the shop as quick as he can.

"That boy is scary," says Millie.

"I know," I say. "Come on, let's pay for our stuff."

When we leave, I want to go straight back to the flat. Being out when Colt could be lurking anywhere jangles my nerves. But Millie insists that we go to the playground and I know it'll be Tantrum City if I refuse. So I'm sitting on the bench while Millie pushes her little fire engine down the slide and explodes with giggles as it flies off the end.

The playground is right in the centre of our bit of the estate, open on all sides. I feel exposed. But Colt wouldn't attack me in broad daylight in front of my little sister. Would he? I fire off a message to Tel, asking what he's doing, but he tells me he's at Lidl with his mum. Huh. You don't hear that from Tony Stark.

I look all around me, up at the landings of the blocks surrounding us. I feel like someone in a war movie, looking out for snipers. I turn around towards Millie to see two figures hopping over the fence on the other side.

"Don't run, we're not here to hurt you," says Jay.

"Yeah, we just want to talk," says Dylan.

If it wasn't for Millie, I could just run, but I'm stuck. They sit on the bench either side of me. My entire body tenses, like I could spring off the bench for a five-metre head start.

"Relax, Finn," says Jay. "We're just here with an invitation."

"No, thanks," I say. "Whatever it is."

"This ain't the kind of invite you turn down," says Dylan.

"Yeah," says Jay. "So you either come with us, or we drag you."

I glance over at Dylan. Jay is small. I'd stand a chance against him, but not Dylan. He looks like he's made of rocks.

"What about my sister?" I say, nodding over at Millie, still happily playing on the slide.

"She can come, too," Jay sniggers. "Make it a family day out." He whistles. "Hey, little one. Fancy a trip?"

"Don't talk to her," I snap. "Where do you want to take us?"

Jay taps the side of his nose. "You'll have to wait until you get there."

Dylan nudges me. "You'll be all right, Finn. It'll be fun." They stand up and look down at me. "Come on, then."

"Millie," I call over to her, trying to seem as calm as possible. "We've got to go now."

"But I don't want to!" she moans.

"I know," I say. "Me neither. But we've got to go with these two."

Millie goes down the slide, but holds on to the side, so it's slow and squeaky. She comes over and I hold her hand.

"Where are we going?" she says.

Jay starts walking off, and Dylan motions for us to follow.

"We're just going to play a game with your brother," Jay says over his shoulder.

"I told you not to talk to her," I say.

Jay giggles. "Someone's touchy."

I look around for anyone I can shout for help to, but there's no one. I reach into my pocket, but Dylan digs me in the ribs. "Don't even think about getting your phone out, mate. Unless you want it smashed."

"Damian, I don't know what's happening," says Millie.

"What did she just call you?" asks Dylan.

I ignore him and squeeze Millie's hand. When is she going to get used to my new name?

They lead us to the garages where I found Millie with Star Kid that night. And we're not alone. Colt is standing in the middle of a semicircle of other kids about our age. All boys. When they see me, a ripple goes around them. I pick out odd comments.

"Is he the best you could find?"

"You'll destroy him!"

I've seen this loads of times before. But I was never one of the people in the middle of the circle. I was always on the outside. And no real fight ever happened because a teacher would always come and break it up. But no teachers are coming now.

I look down at Millie, still holding tight to her little toys. "Hey, Mils," I say. "Do you remember how to get to Gino's where Mummy works?"

She takes her thumb out with a pop. "I think so."

"Would you be able to run there really fast?"

She looks at me like I suggested sprouting wings and flying. "On myself?"

"Yes," I say.

"But I'm not supposed to. I'll get in trouble."

"It's OK just this once."

"Oi!" Colt shouts across. "What you waiting for?"

I squeeze Millie's hand. "Run," I whisper.

She takes a deep breath, puffs out her chest, then takes off in the direction we came.

"Should we go after her?" asks Dylan.

"Leave it," says Jay. "This won't take long." He shoves me and I stumble further into the semicircle, which starts to draw into a tight ring.

"Thought you could hide from me for ever, Finn?" asks Colt. His eyes are blank, like a shark's.

"Stop talking and hit him, Colt!" someone shouts, and everyone else cheers.

I could try and escape. I could force my way through and run and run until I find shelter. But I can't do that. I've got to go to that school in September. They'll eat me alive. I've got to stand my ground.

Colt shoves me. "Come on, then. Take a swing. Dare you."

This would never have happened back home. I was a Butcher. That meant something. Now who am I?

"Smack him, Colt!"

I don't even know how to fight. I've never had to. In all that time I never asked myself if I wanted to.

He shoves me again. "Well, come on, then. Not so hard now your mate isn't here, are you?"

He's right: I wish Tel was here. He'd know what to do.

Something hits my back, sending warm liquid fizzing over my neck and on to my head. I shudder. The circle cheers and I look down to see a bottle of Pepsi splurting out the last of its contents. OW! Something's hit the back of my head, and it's lit up in pain, and I feel myself pitching forward, crashing to the ground. I roll myself on to my back and try to scramble away, but he's grabbing at my legs and the back of my head hurts and he's on top of me and he's stronger than I thought he'd be and he's grabbing my collar and I'm trying to stop him but I can't and he's making my head bounce off the ground and it really hurts and everyone is standing over us and cheering and I cry out for him to stop but he won't and kicking my legs does nothing and I hear a voice and it's a voice I know and it's saying "Get off him" and Colt is gone and I stagger to my feet and everyone is running away and Dad has Colt around the neck and he's screaming in his face and Colt looks terrified and Dad is threatening him and he's saying if you ever go near my son again I will break your neck, and I'm feeling that old rush of power I used to feel and I hate myself for it, I hate myself, I hate myself, I hate myself, but I'm relieved that Dad arrived when he did but now he's walking towards me and I can tell I'm not out of the woods yet.

CHAPTER 17

We walk home in silence. Not even Millie speaks. My head is throbbing. Dad walks fast and I struggle to keep up. I don't know why he isn't at work or where Millie found him, but I can't ask.

Dad fumbles with his key in the lock and swears under his breath as he struggles to turn it, but when it does, he throws the door open, making it smack against the wall. When it's slammed shut, he turns on me.

"What happened?" His eyes are wide and his breathing is short. I've seen him like this before. It never ends well.

"He was just being an id-idiot," I say, my voice coming out pathetic and wobbly.

"Why didn't you fight back?" he says, not even listening.

"I-I tried, he was just—"

Dad still isn't listening. He's walking away, still fizzing with anger. I can almost smell it coming off him. Where's he going? It sounds like he's gone into our bedroom. I look at Millie. She's sitting on the sofa, staring at the TV, even though it isn't on.

"Get in here," he shouts.

I do as I'm told. He's standing by my bed with a load of Tel's comics bunched in his fist.

"I've been soft on you for too long," he says. "It's time you grew up."

Rrrrrrrrip. He tears two in half at the same time.

"No!" I yell. "They're not even mine!"

Dad rips another and throws the pieces on the floor. "Everything I did, Damian, it was for you, you know that?"

I don't know what to say, and even if I did, I know my voice would come out weak and that would make him worse.

"Everything I did was to protect you, you understand me?" he growls, ripping another comic. "So you wouldn't go the same way I did. But now, I can't do it, can I? So that means you have to step up. You've got to learn to stand up for yourself."

He holds a comic at arm's length, his thick fingers creasing the pages. "Come on, then. Stop me."

But I don't do anything. My head throbs harder and – I don't want to, I really don't want to – I fight it like hell, but I'm crying. Dad throws down the comics and comes after me. I turn away and cover my face.

"This is my son? This is who is supposed to continue the Butcher family name?"

I want to say there *is* no Butcher family name. That it ended because of him, but I can't.

"You're a man," he growls. "Stop crying."

I want to. I want to stop more than anything in the world, but I can't. And it's not just because of Tel's comics. It's because deep down I know he's right. I'm not hard. I don't like sports. I think about stuff too much. I'm doing it right now. I'm not a real man.

Dad storms out and slams the door behind him and I fall down on my bed. I hear the door open again, but I can tell from the lightness of the footsteps that it isn't Dad. I feel a little hand on my back.

"If you want to cry, it's OK, Damian," I hear Millie say. Then she leans in and whispers in my ear. "Daddy's mean."

I sit up, wipe my eyes and give her a hug. I'm glad she's not going to be expected to be like him, too.

"I got lost trying to find Mummy and I saw Daddy in the car park," says Millie. "He was angry because I was on myself."

I run my hands through my hair and let out a shaky sigh. What a mess. Before I can start with the trademark Finn overthinking, I grab my phone and text Tel.

You see, I realized something when I was forced into that fight: that the mask I've been wearing my whole life is off.

It's time to put on a new one.

CHAPTER 18

Star Kid paces backwards and forwards around the back of the community centre. I'm in my Moon Boy costume, and even though it's eleven thirty at night, I still feel like I'm being watched.

"OK, Moon Boy," he says. "This is a crash course in superhero-dom, so listen up."

I salute him sarcastically, but he's too busy pacing to catch it.

"Now you might have watched movies and flipped through my comics," he says.

About that...

"But they are not real life," Star Kid goes on. "We do not have superpowers, nor do we have billion-dollar technology. All we have to go on is what's in here." He taps the side of his head.

"So let's start with the basics: self-defence. In this line of work, people are liable to attack you."

"Have you ever been attacked?" I ask, then remember what happened with Colt and the others. "As Star Kid, I mean."

"Well … no. Some little rotter threw a bottle of strawberry milk at me last week, but that's about it. Nevertheless, you have to always be prepared."

"OK," I say. "So what do I do?"

I'm keen to learn. If what happened with Colt proved anything, it's that I have zero self-defence skills. I haven't told Tel about what happened. I don't even want to think about it. I just want to be prepared if it happens again.

"A lot of it is down to how you carry yourself," says Star Kid. "You have to command any space you enter. Walk with your head held high and your shoulders back. If you look scared, they'll sense it."

I do as he says. Weirdly, I do kind of feel more confident.

"Good." Star Kid nods briskly. "Now, secondly, you have to be light on your feet. If someone's coming at you, you can't be caught flat-footed."

He goes up on his tiptoes and bounces a little. "Now I'm ready to move off in any direction in a split second. You try."

I do as he says, but I'm not used to the boots and I stumble into him.

"OK," says Star Kid, gently pushing me back. "Not bad for a first go. Try again."

This attempt goes a bit better.

"Good," says Star Kid. "Next thing: now we're a duo, we have a whole new world of combat available to us, but let's take things slow and start off with a classic: the old all-fours push-over."

I frown. "You mean when one of us gets on our hands and knees behind someone and the other one pushes them over?"

"Exactly!" says Star Kid. "So when I say, 'Assume the position', you drop to the ground behind the perpetrator and I'll take care of the rest."

"Seems easy enough, I suppose."

"It certainly does," says Star Kid. "Now, I can't teach you everything I know about fighting. It took me years. But if you can defend yourself, that's half the battle. Leave the heavy stuff to me. You're the sidekick, after all."

"Hold on a sec," I say. "Sidekick? I didn't agree to that. I thought we were equal partners."

"There's no shame in being a sidekick," says Star Kid. "Some of the best superheroes of all time started off that way: Nightwing … Winter Soldier … um … Harley Quinn."

"Isn't she a villain?" I ask.

"Look, let's not get bogged down in semantics. Your sidekick status isn't important. What is important is our mission."

"Which is?" I ask.

Star Kid stops pacing and stands square in front of me. "Well, our long-term mission is to make Ampleforth a better place to live."

"OK," I say. "So that means there's a short-term one?"

Star Kid steps closer to me. "Yes. But it's a big one." He seems a little tense.

"And what is it?" I ask.

Star Kid takes a deep breath. "If we are going to make Ampleforth a better place to live, we have to do one big thing. It's a thing I've been wanting to do for years. Probably the entire reason I started learning jiu-jitsu and designing costumes." He hesitates.

"Go on," I say.

"We are going to bring down Ronnie."

Oh. That is a big one.

"OK," I say. "Why?"

"He's dangerous," says Star Kid, his voice low and

full of anger. "He's a blight. He's a leech. Ronnie has to go for the good of every single Ampleforth resident."

"But how are we supposed to do it?"

"I'm not sure yet," says Star Kid. "But with two of us on the mission, it's going to be more achievable."

I think back to the only time I've seen him. Everyone seems terrified of him. How are we supposed to get rid of him?

"I don't know if we're going to be able to do that, Tel," I say.

"First off: no real names, Moon Boy. And second, yes we will. It will be a big change for the estate, but change can be good. I mean, listen to me. Do you think I grew up talking like this?"

I think about it. He is far and away the poshest person around here. Around anywhere, to be honest.

"Of course I didn't. But when you look like me, and come from this estate, and are raised by a single parent, people will make assumptions about you, so I educated myself, and I learned to speak with precision. Has it won me any friends? Of course it hasn't. But I'm used to proving people wrong, Moon Boy, so when I say we're going to bring down Ronnie, I mean it."

I want to tell him that people like Ronnie are different: that they won't go quietly, that they'll do anything they can to survive, that I know people like Ronnie, that I grew up around people like Ronnie, that a person like Ronnie makes up half of my DNA, but I can't, so I say nothing.

"So here's what I know about Ronnie from my surveillance," Star Kid goes on.

"Surveillance?"

"I follow him around sometimes," he says. "Anyway, he lives over there." He points across the road at a single-row street. "See those two houses in the middle? He owns both of them."

"Why does he need two houses?" I ask.

"He doesn't," says Star Kid. "But he's knocked it through to one big house, anyway. Probably to show how superior he is to all of us. It makes me want to vomit."

"Well, it's not as if we can just march in there and demand he turns himself in to the police cos he's got two houses," I say.

"I'm aware of that," says Star Kid. "But I just need you to understand that he's our target, our white whale, our Thanos, our Joker. Understand?"

"I think so," I say.

"That's what I like to hear, Moon Boy," he says with a smile. "Now come on, I've got to teach you some takedowns. I hope you don't bruise easily."

CHAPTER 19

Two whole days after my superhero training, I'm still sore, but I'm trying not to make it too obvious. I feel good in other ways. I feel stronger; I feel useful.

Mum brought some food from the café home for dinner. It smells delicious. We're not allowed to touch it, though. We have to wait for Dad to get home. I wish we didn't. I've barely spoken to him since he ripped up Tel's comics, despite him trying to act like it didn't happen. How am I supposed to come clean about what happened? Those things could be worth serious money for all I know.

"Now, this is our little secret, OK?" says Mum. "Let's have Daddy believe I cooked this at home."

The door opens and Dad walks in.

"Good evening, family!" he says, all chirpy. He comes in, kisses Millie on the head, ruffles my hair and gives Mum a hug.

"Someone's in a good mood," says Mum.

Dad sits at the table, a satisfied smile on his face. "How could I not be, coming home to such a wonderful family? And this dinner? It looks stupendous!"

Stupendous? Since when does he say stupendous?

"It's prawn linguine," says Mum.

Dad starts digging in with his fork, then stops. "Linguine? Isn't that Italian?"

"Well, yes," says Mum.

Dad stares for a second, the smile frozen on his face. "Did what's-his-name teach you to make it?"

"Gino?" says Mum. "Well, it's going to be on the menu at the café, so he kind of had to. Anyway, enough about that." I notice her voice going wobbly. "Eat it before it goes cold."

Dad puts down his fork. "Maybe I'm not hungry."

"Oh, don't be like that," says Mum.

"Like what?" he snaps. "How am I being?"

"Dad." It slips out of my mouth before I can stop it. Straight away, his eyes are on me. It's the unwritten family rule that we don't get involved when Mum and Dad are having one of their "discussions".

"You got something to say?" says Dad.

"You know the other day?" I say, trying to keep my voice breezy.

Dad's stare hardens and I try not to shrivel under it like a slug covered in salt. Neither of us have spoken to Mum about what happened. I could have, but I don't want to cause even more upset.

"What about it?" His voice is as cold and sharp as a knife.

"How come you weren't at work?"

Any hint of friendliness vanishes from his face, but I don't look away, even though I really want to. If he wants me to be a man, he should be careful what he wishes for.

"I don't know what you're talking about."

"When that kid was trying to start a fight with me, and you broke it up," I say.

"Hold on," says Mum. "What's this fight? Damia—Finn, you never told me about that!"

Dad's face cracks into a grin as he turns to her and says, "Oh, just a little scuffle. Boys being boys." Then he turns back to me, once again stone-faced.

"If you must know, the plant went down so we

were allowed to go home early," he says. "And it's lucky for you it did, because if I wasn't there, who knows what would have happened?"

I don't know if he's telling the truth or not. He's too good a liar. Dad chuckles warmly, ruffles my hair so hard it hurts, then reaches into his pocket and slides a tenner across the table.

"You're a good boy, Finn. How about you go out and buy yourself some of those baby comics you like? Replace the ones that got damaged?"

He picks up his fork and twirls a big ball of pasta, still smiling.

"That got damaged?" I repeat. The way he said it makes it seem like an accident.

"You're a very good boy," he says, winking at me. "Now enough with the silly questions, OK?"

CHAPTER 20

It's ten thirty on the dot when the taps come. I'm already dressed and ready to go. Star Kid grins when I hop out of the window.

"Looking stylish as ever, Moon Boy." He's speaking in his normal voice, which I'm glad about because that would have sounded weird as Star Kid.

This is my first official patrol as Moon Boy and I'm trying not to make it obvious that I'm nervous. Is this such a great idea? I know I agreed to do it after the fight, but that was then. Maybe I've calmed down now.

We head down the stairs and across the car park. It's a stuffy night and I'm already starting to sweat. This suit doesn't have much breathing room.

"So have you seen those two blokes by the community centre since last week?" I ask him.

"Nope," he says. "I reckon we scared them off. The power of Sunbeam!"

Sure enough, when we get to the community centre, there's no one there. In fact, the whole area is deserted.

OK, if there's nothing going on, I'm going to have to tell him about the comics. It'll have to come out eventually.

"I, uh, have a confession to make," I say.

Star Kid slaps his hands either side of his face. "You're secretly working for Ronnie?"

I know he's joking, but it makes me uncomfortable. "No, it's about your comics," I say.

Star Kid looks surprised. "They were too difficult for you?"

"No, I…" I can't look at him. "My, um, sister was playing and she, well, she put them in the bath. I'm sorry."

It's the best I could come up with.

Tel tuts and rolls his eyes. "See, this is why I only gave you duplicates. I knew a reprobate like you couldn't be trusted with the good ones."

Relief washes over me like a warm shower. I expected him to flip out.

"OK, now confession time is over, can we get back to our patrol?"

My heart rate is beginning to slow as we walk across the precinct.

"I've got a question for you," I say.

"Proceed," says Star Kid.

"What happens if nothing happens?"

"Come again?"

"What do we do if there are no crimes or anything like that?"

"HELP!"

The scream comes from around the back of the community centre. We take off down the path. It's probably someone messing about. But as we get closer, I hear the sounds of struggling.

Adrenaline surges through my body so fast I somehow forget how out of breath I am. We round the corner and see three shadowy figures tussling. It's only when we get closer that I see it's an old lady and two lads trying to take her bags.

"Stop!" Star Kid booms.

They look up at us and freeze.

"Chuffing Nora!" the old lady, who I now realize is Pat from the food bank, gasps.

Star Kid charges them and they scatter in two different directions.

"Moon Boy, you take that one," he says, pointing

at the kid that's running down the left-hand alley. The kid sprints into the precinct, past Ali's. I'm wondering how I'm ever going to catch him when, *THONK*, he runs straight into a bollard, making impact with it in a place which must be incredibly painful. Oh. I'd feel bad for him if he hadn't just been trying to mug a pensioner.

Ali comes out of the shop and sees me standing over him.

"What's going on here?" he says.

"The little thug was trying to snatch my handbag," says Pat, who had followed us round.

"Is that so?" says Ali, pulling the lad to his feet and making him cry out in pain. "Well, we'll see what the police have to say about that, won't we?" He nods at me. "Thanks ... whoever you are."

I could explain that it's actually his bollard that deserves the credit, but he's bundling the thief into the shop.

Before long, Star Kid appears with the other one. He has his arm twisted behind his back.

"Now are you going to say sorry to Pat?" he growls.

"Sorry!" the thief pants.

"This lady runs the food bank, and gives her free

time to this community and this is how you repay her?" says Star Kid.

The lad whimpers something, then kicks Star Kid in the shin, making him cry out and lose his grip. The lad takes off towards Ali's and, with impeccable timing, does exactly the same thing his mate did.

"Well, they didn't exactly send their best and brightest, did they?" says Pat.

We stay and watch them getting carted away by the police.

"All in a day's work," says Star Kid, proudly.

Pat, who is absolutely fine and obviously hard as nails, nudges me. "So, who are you two, anyway?"

"We are Star Kid and Moon Boy," says Star Kid. "The Ampleforth Avengers." Then, after a dramatic pause, he digs me in the ribs with his elbow. "'What if nothing happens?' You're adorable."

I climb back in through the window, buzzing with excitement. It feels like we really achieved something tonight, something worthwhile, something—

"AAAAAAAARRGH!"

The scream makes me jump so high, I nearly bounce off the ceiling.

No, no, no, Millie is awake, Millie is awake, this is

code red!

I quickly rip off my mask.

"Mils!" I whisper. "It's OK, it's just me, Finn."

Millie is crying softly. "I was scared. I thought you were a monster."

"What's going on in there?" Dad snaps from the hall.

"Millie's just had a nightmare!" I call back, pulling the costume off as fast as I can.

"Finn, what are you doing?" Millie says. "Why have you got those clothes on? Where have you been?"

"I'm just playing," I say. "I'm being silly!"

Millie seems to be calming down. I quickly throw on my pyjamas and sit on her bed.

"It's OK," I whisper, putting my arm around her. "I'm not a monster."

Millie gently snivels into my shoulder. "I heard Mummy and Daddy shouting the other night and Mummy said something about bad people looking for Daddy. I thought it was a bad people."

I close my eyes. It's so unfair that she has to know about things like that.

"The bad people are very far away," I say. "They're not going to find us."

I don't tell her that none of us really know where

Uncle Shane is. He could be anywhere in the world, and that's something we're going to have to live with until he's found.

Millie sniffs loudly and her breath revs.

"That's why I was dressed up like that," I say. "So if the bad people show up, I can stop them, and no one will know it was me."

"Really?"

"Yeah," I say. "But you can't tell Mummy or Daddy. It has to be our secret."

"OK," Millie croaks.

"Promise?"

Millie nods.

I don't get back into bed until Millie's asleep. Great. I couldn't even manage a full day as a superhero without my secret identity being found out. Bruce Wayne I ain't.

Worry Book

Millie's old enough to know what secrets are, right?

CHAPTER 21

I'm heading out with Dad. We're having a chippy tea tonight and he's insisted I come with him to pick it up.

On the way down the stairs, he hits me with a play punch. "You're quiet, son."

"Am I?" I mumble.

"What's up? Your girlfriend dump you?"

He knows I don't have a girlfriend. He just likes to bring it up so he can say—

"When I was your age, I was fighting them off with a stick."

Right on cue.

As we get outside, he puts a hand on my shoulder to stop me. I sigh. I don't even want to be here, let alone talk to him.

"Look, son," he says. "That was wrong of me. You know, what I did the other day. I shouldn't have ripped up your comics."

YOU DON'T SAY.

"I just worry about you, that's all," he says, cupping my face. "Especially now. Cos I know people left you alone back home, but they're not going to here. You can't be soft in this world, or people will walk all over you."

I say nothing. I don't even want to look at him. I focus my eyes on a thin strip of sky between his face and Ambrose Court. Blues melting into pinks, with a fine cloud lazily hanging over it like a cobweb.

"And if anything happens to me, you'll be the man of the house," he goes on. "And men have to be strong, OK?"

I keep staring at the sky and nod a little. Dad taps my cheek gently. "There's a good lad."

When we get to the precinct, the queue for the chippy is out the door. Ali is standing outside his shop, chatting with a couple of old blokes.

"I swear to you, I thought they were ninjas," he says. "They took off after these hooligans, well I say 'they' – one of them was much quicker than the other – but honestly, I've never seen anything like it."

Dad shoots me a look. "What are you smiling at?"

Oh. I didn't realize I was. "Nothing. Just remembered a funny joke."

Dad chuckles. "Oh yeah? Why don't you tell me?"

I frantically search my memory for a joke, any joke, and come away empty-handed. Come on, there has to be something. Why did the chicken cross the road? Will he buy that? He won't let it go until I tell him, I know he won't.

"Hey, Chris!"

Oh, thank you, random stranger. The bloke in front of us in the queue has turned around. I don't know how he knows Dad, but right now I don't care. The heat is off me.

"Luke," Dad replies, his voice flat.

"How you doing, mate?" says the bloke. He's got this overstretched smile on his face, so wide it's practically wobbling.

"All right," says Dad.

It goes quiet. The jolly mask Dad had slipped on for our little trip has gone.

"Tell you what," says the bloke, still grinning, "you go ahead of me. I'm not in a rush."

Dad gives him a thin smile and nods, then steps

around the man. To begin with, I don't want to follow, but it looks like I have no choice. I glance at Dad to see if he's going to explain, but it doesn't look like it.

That chippy smell wafts out of the open door, making my mouth water, despite everything. Man, I'm starving.

Dad aims a playful, slow-motion punch at my head and starts bobbing and weaving. "Come on, put 'em up," he says. Looks like the mask is back on.

I roll my eyes, just like Tel would, but Dad hits me with another jab. "Got you again. Come on, show me what you've got."

He puts his hands up, palms outwards. "Hard as you can."

I hit his hand with a pretty good punch, but Dad just laughs. "Ooh, did a fly just land on me? Try again, and this time put some welly into it."

I hit him harder, but he just shakes his head and looks at the guy in the queue behind us. "Kids these days," he says. "I blame computer games." The bloke laughs like he's been told the brilliant joke I lied about remembering.

Dad grabs me in a headlock and rubs his knuckles across my scalp. I hate it when he does that.

"So, have you heard about these superheroes

doing the rounds?" he says, when he finally lets me go.

I use the distraction of rubbing my burning head to cover for the fact that I'm freaking out. "Superheroes?"

"Yeah," he says. "Everyone's talking about them."

"Really?" I croak.

"Yeah," he says. "People say they look about your age. I bet you know them. Especially with you being into all that make-believe comic stuff now."

I swallow hard. "I doubt it," I say. "I don't know any real superheroes."

Dad laughs. "Apart from your old man, of course."

Sure.

When we get inside the chippy, George, the bloke who runs it, gives Dad a thumbs up. "Hey, Chris!" he says. "Great to see you, mate." He taps the shoulder of the lady who's with him behind the counter. "Debbie, fry my friend Chris here up a fresh cod, will you?"

I look up at Dad and he winks. "How about that, son? Fresh cod."

Worry Book

Was it obvious I was lying about not knowing about the superheroes?

Why are people treating Dad like they did back home?

CHAPTER 22

As Star Kid and I pass the community centre, my mind drifts. I'm sure we didn't have a community centre in our old neighbourhood. There wasn't a single place everyone went to do stuff. Everyone just did their own thing, pretty much. Well, Dad, Uncle Shane and the rest had that pub they always hung out in. Every now and then, Dad would take me down there, then spend most of his time making fun of me in front of his friends or beating me at pool. I don't miss that.

It's a quiet, still night with no breeze. It reminds me of those holidays we used to go on once, sometimes twice a year, to places like Spain and Greece. Now those I do miss. I wonder if we'll ever get to go to places like that again.

Shouting and whooping drifts down from the other end of the estate. Star Kid shakes his head. "Even though I'm aware that the full moon is nothing but a lunar event," he says, "I still can't shake the idea that it brings out the weirdos."

The fact that he said this while we're both walking around in rubber outfits doesn't seem to strike him as weird, so I let it go.

We take a different route tonight, going past the precinct and heading into the streets, before looping back and ending where we started.

"So, have you found any more candidates for the team?" I ask Star Kid.

He shakes his head. "Not yet, but one should always live in hope. I'm thinking I'd quite like a powerhouse. You know, like the Hulk? Because I have the agility and the fighting skill, and you've got..." He hesitates. "You've got determination, so we need something we don't already have covered."

"Well, if I see any big green blokes, I'll let you know," I say, trying to shrug off the painful fact that I obviously have no special skills whatsoever.

We walk quietly, listening out for any signs of action. The streets are confusing around here. Back home, they would be clearly marked; long tree-lined roads with road signs. Here, the streets intersect and zigzag. Sometimes, you'll be walking down a cycle path with two rows of houses from separate streets directly facing each other on either side. We're walking down one of these now. Lots of people have their windows open, so I can hear TVs and talking and laughing.

Up ahead, there's a group of older kids in the underpass. Now, if I were on my own, there's no way I'd walk through them. Not here. Back home would be a different story because they'd know not to mess with me. But right here, right now, I want to go any other way but this one. Star Kid isn't flinching, though.

"Look, it's the superheroes!" one of them hoots.

Here we go.

Most of the kids are taller than us and stand huddled around each other, hands crammed into hoodie pockets.

"I love you, lads; can we have a selfie?" a girl asks.

Hold on a sec. Are they mocking us? I scan their faces for any hint of sarcasm as we enter the underpass, but I can't detect any.

"I don't see why not," says Star Kid.

"Ooh, listen to his voice! It's like Batman!"

They all crowd around us and take selfies, posing and laughing. Man, is this what it feels like to be a celebrity? When they've finally taken enough, they let us carry on, with plenty of backslaps and "Good on ya"s thrown in.

"Word is spreading, Phineas," says Star Kid, a little smile on his lips.

"I know," I say. "My dad asked me about it the other day."

His head snaps around so fast, it's like he's being attacked by an invisible ninja.

"Really? What did you say?"

"Relax!" I say. "I denied all knowledge, obviously."

Star Kid nods. "Good. We have to keep this totally secret. Especially from parents."

"Doesn't your mum suspect anything?" I ask him.

"She's too busy. Just works and sleeps most of the time," he says.

It occurs to me we've never really talked about his family. Maybe I should ask. Show a bit of interest. "So are your parents divorced or something?"

His mouth tightens. "Dad's not around." The way he says it feels like he doesn't want to talk about it any more. I should probably leave it.

"OI!"

The yell comes from somewhere near the precinct. Star Kid takes off down the path and I follow. It's probably nothing. Like Star Kid said, it's a full moon. But as we get closer, it's obvious it isn't. A figure in a black balaclava is sprinting away from Ali's and off into the estate.

Ali, breathless and sweaty, runs after him but can't keep up. "Get back here, you little toerag!" he puffs.

He looks over at us and does a double take.

"Perfect timing!" he says. "Get after him, will you?"

Star Kid starts running in the same direction as the shoplifter, and I join him.

About a minute later, I start getting a stitch. Oh man, I wish I'd tried harder in cross-country instead of just strolling around the field. Running is hard enough as it is without being dressed in a rubber suit.

We stop in a patch of grass surrounded by houses. I'm glad of the chance to catch my breath. "Listen!" says Star Kid.

I try to, but my own ragged breaths and thudding pulse are all I can hear. There's a scuffling sound coming from an alley between two rows opposite us and Star Kid takes off that way.

"It might just have been a cat!" I rasp after him, but it's no use. By the time I get to the alley, I hear two pairs of feet scurrying around.

"Give yourself up!" Star Kid yells. "You're only making things harder for yourself."

It's at this point I realize it's not just an alley, but a rabbit warren of criss-crossing walkways that's like a really grubby hedge maze.

"Who designed this place?" I wonder aloud.

I stagger along in the dark, trying to figure out where Star Kid is when WHAM. I fall to the ground with another body tumbling on top of me. In the sickly orange light of the lamp post, I can see it's the shoplifter.

"S-stop," I say, wrapping my arms around him.

He tries to wriggle free, but I tighten my grip.

"Star Kid!" I yell. "I've got him. For now, anyway."

I hear Star Kid arrive and lift the shoplifter off me. I scramble to my feet. Star Kid is pressing him against the wall.

"What the hell are you two?" The shoplifter sounds terrified. And familiar. Really familiar.

Star Kid grabs the balaclava and pulls it off.

"Colt!" I blurt out.

"How do you know my name?" he says.

Oh yeah. Good point.

"Never mind that." Star Kid shoots me a look. "What did you take?"

"Nothing," says Colt.

"Look, if we sweep the area, we'll find whatever it is you ditched, so you might as well just tell us."

Colt's eyes dart from side to side. "All right," he says. "I took a couple of tins of soup and some beans, OK?"

Star Kid loosens his grip and lets Colt stand freely. "That all?"

"Yeah, I swear! Ronnie has had the last of our money. We've got nothing to eat!"

"What do you mean, he's had the last of your money?" asks Star Kid.

"My dad owed him," says Colt. "He wouldn't take no for an answer."

Star Kid looks at me, his mouth turned downwards, then back at Colt.

"Here's what you're going to do. First thing tomorrow, you're going down to the community centre and you're seeing Pat at the food bank. She will take care of you. You do not steal food from Ali ever again, do you understand me?"

"Yes!" Colt whimpers. "I'm sorry."

"What Ronnie is doing is wrong. And we are going to stop him, I promise," Star Kid says. "But you need to start being nicer to people," Star Kid growls. "I've been watching you. And if I find out you haven't done what I've said, we will come back for you, do you understand?"

"Yes!" Colt says.

"Good. Now get out of my sight."

Colt runs away into the night, leaving me staring at Star Kid in amazement.

"You could have shopped him to the police," I say. "Why didn't you?"

"That isn't what this is about, Phineas," says Star Kid. "We're not about punishment, we're about doing what's right. We're going to find the food and return it to Ali and say nothing. Besides, Colt's not the real problem; Ronnie is. He's a human leech. He's got to go."

I blink hard and shake my head to try and stop myself thinking about how many people like Colt would have been affected by what Dad and Uncle Shane were doing, and how it paid for our house and all my stuff.

"So how are we going to do it?" I ask, desperately stamping the thoughts into the dirt.

"I don't know," says Star Kid. "But we need to think of something. And fast."

CHAPTER 23

It's late afternoon and me, Mum and Millie are sitting quietly, watching TV. I feel like we're all mentally preparing for Dad to come home, just like we've had to do every day lately. When you never know how someone is going to behave, it's like being told you're going to get a present, but it's a toss-up between it being a teddy bear or a grenade. My phone vibrates. Message from Tel.

> Just received a tip-off about something that's going to be on the news in five mins. Put it on.

Luckily, *Amazing Kids* with Casey Kellman is coming to an end, so I grab the remote and slyly change the channel. It's the local news showing a report about a burst water main somewhere posh, causing flooding.

"Why have you put this on, Finn?" asks Mum.

I shrug. "Just thought it would be a change."

"It's boring," Mille moans.

It cuts back to the newsreader in the studio: an older man who is grinning a twinkly-eyed grin. "Would-be muggers on an estate in Tammerstone were thwarted by two masked vigilantes on Wednesday night in an amazing, and eventually hilarious, rescue. Gary Duffy has more."

When the camera shows the community centre, Millie shrieks with joy. "Look, Mummy! That's where I go to day care!"

I lean forward so I can hear. "When Pat Hodgkins was leaving her volunteer job at the food bank late on Wednesday night, she was accosted by two young men."

The camera shows Pat standing outside the community centre. "Well, I couldn't believe it," she says. "I've lived on this estate for thirty years and nothing like this has ever happened to me before."

"What did they want?" the reporter asks.

"They were trying to snatch my bag, and I wasn't giving it up without a fight. I had all the cash donations for the food bank in it, and no snotty little thugs were going to take that away."

The camera then shows Pat being attacked on CCTV. My heart races, my skin prickles.

"Poor Pat," says Mum.

Then, you see Star Kid and Moon Boy run in and the two muggers run away. At the very top of the screen, the kid I'm chasing runs crotch-first into the bollard, which makes Mum scream with laughter. When the other one comes back and does the same thing, she's almost crying.

"I'm so grateful to those two young men," says Pat.

The camera cuts to close-ups of our masked faces taken from the CCTV. "There is a tight-knit community here in Tammerstone, and with these two superheroes looking out for them, the residents can sleep a little safer at night. Gary Duffy, Mercian News in Tammerstone."

Mum is still laughing, but Millie is dead silent and staring right at me, her eyes wide like saucers.

"Mum," I say. "Me and Millie are just going to nip to the shop."

Mum is still giggling. She's like that when something really gets her. "OK," she says, "but be back in ten minutes."

I get Millie ready and hurry her out of the door.

"You're a superhero!" she yells.

"Shhh!" I say, looking around to make sure no one can hear her. "It's a secret, remember?"

"You know Star Kid!"

I nod. "He asked me to join his team, OK?"

"That's so cool!" says Millie.

We quickly leave the block and head towards the precinct. "You must not tell *anyone*," I say. "Not Mum, definitely not Dad, not anyone at day care. *No one*."

Millie sticks her bottom lip out. "But I want to tell everyone! None of my friends at day care have superhero brothers."

"I know," I say. "But if you do tell anyone, then I won't be able to be a superhero any more. It has to stay a secret."

We're outside the shop now. Millie folds her arms, still pouting. "OK," she says.

"Great," I say. "Now how about we go and get you some Cherry Zingas?"

The pouting immediately stops. "YAYYYY!"

CHAPTER 24

"You know what we have to do, don't you?" says Star Kid.

We're walking across the bridge over the dual carriageway. The same one Colt took me to on his "tour". It's dark and the road below is a blur of whizzing headlights. I've decided not to tell him that Millie knows. She's not going to say anything, and even if she does, she's four. The other week, she was going around telling everyone we'd travelled to Tammerstone from the planet Zoozlebum.

"No, I don't actually," I say.

"We need to get evidence of Ronnie's wrongdoings. Hard evidence."

"And how are we going to do that?" I ask. "He

seems pretty private. It's not like he goes around advertising what he's up to, is it?"

Star Kid rubs his chin. "In an ideal world, one of us would infiltrate his organization, go undercover. But Ronnie's going to be really suspicious of anyone approaching him to join his gang. We need to think creatively."

I look over the edge of the bridge as brake lights burn red in the dark. How did they get Dad and all his gang? They were doing what they wanted for years and the police couldn't pin anything on them. How did they make anything stick? Ah, that's it!

"We could bug him," I say.

"Bug him?"

"Hide a mic somewhere when he's having a meeting. If he says anything – what's the word? – *incriminating*, we can pass the recording on to the police."

Star Kid grins and whacks my arm. "Very nice, Phineas. What made you think of that?"

I shrug. "Saw it on a TV show." I don't tell him that police bugged the pub Dad, Uncle Shane and all the others used to meet in. Hid a mic in the light above a pool table and caught them discussing a load of bad stuff. If they hadn't done that, I wouldn't be here right now. I'd be back home, in my own bed, in my own room.

Star Kid takes his phone out of his belt and googles bugging devices. The cheapest one is forty quid. He has a savings account and I offer him the tenner Dad gave me.

"Where does he meet people?" I ask.

"From what I can tell, they go to him, at his house. Real rogues' gallery of charmers, barely a set of teeth between them," says Star Kid. "I've never seen him talk to anyone anywhere else."

"So we have to get a bug into his house," I say. "How are we going to do that?"

"We'll find a way," says Star Kid. He looks at me for a second, before smiling and clapping me on the shoulder. "Bugging him! Why didn't I think of that? You're a genius, Moon Boy."

I blush. No one's ever called me a genius before. Mainly because I'm not one, but it's still nice.

Worry Book

Tel won't think it's weird that I came up with the bugging idea so easily, will he?

CHAPTER 25

Ah, those blissful few seconds when I wake up and forget where I am. Sometimes they're the best seconds of the day.

Then I turn over and see Millie lying in her bed staring at me and sucking her thumb and I remember. I'm in Ampleforth. Great.

I pick up my phone. There's a message from Tel. Man, it was sent at four o'clock in the morning!

Isn't coffee WONDERFUL? I'd never really bothered with it before, but now I am INTO IT. Anyway, don't be mad, but I was up late ordering our bugging device when I was seized with inspiration and I did something. Here's the link:

Oh, here we go. I click the link and a website loads up.

**STAR KID AND MOON BOY: THE
AMPLEFORTH AVENGERS**

**Got a problem? Report it here!
You can remain anonymous.**

It's pretty basic: just a black background and white text with a drawing of us. Underneath, there's a box people can fill in. I go back to my messages. There's more.

> I thought it might encourage some people to report Ronnie. You know, off the record. It would go well with the bugging thing. What do you think?

I text back, at least relieved he hasn't included a real photo of me on the site.

> Yeah, good.

A reply comes straight away.

Good. Good. Because I handmade some
stickers with the URL on and am currently
going around the estate sticking them to
things.

How are you still awake??

What's keeping me awake is JUSTICE,
Phineas. Also, as I mentioned before, coffee.
Lots of coffee.

I get dressed and walk into the lounge. Mum and Dad
are already up. Dad has put music on in the kitchen,
and I can tell it was him, because it's that rock station
he always listens to. I catch a glimpse of them as I pass
the door. They're dancing and Mum is laughing. I'm
just relieved they're not arguing again.

I sit on the sofa and switch on the TV. Millie runs
in and jumps on to the seat next to me.

"You don't have to follow me everywhere, Mils,"
I say.

"I don't like being on my own," she huffs. "It's
scary."

Dad leans into the lounge. "Oh, my children are
awake! Good morning!"

I don't know why he's in such a good mood.

"And what are you up to today?"

I was planning to lounge around the flat, but something about his mood is weirding me out. I've seen it before. The fake cheeriness is always a cover for something else.

"Might just go out with my friend," I say.

"Is it your super friend?" says Millie.

I freeze, and my mouth drops open. Dad raises his eyebrows at me.

"Which super friend is this?" he asks. "Nothing to do with that lad I spoke to, is he?"

"N-no," I stammer. "It's a different friend."

Luckily, this seems to be enough for Dad and he chuckles. "Well, have fun, OK?" He reaches into his back pocket and pulls out a big wodge of cash, peels off a couple of notes and passes them to me.

"Where did you get all that?" asks Mum, coming up behind Dad.

Dad shrugs. "Got a bonus at work. Employee of the week."

There's a look on Mum's face I can't quite work out. It seems to move from happy to confused to worried before settling on something that seems like a combination of the three.

"Great!" she says. "Well, it's nice to see you're getting on with your boss now."

Dad smirks. "We're getting on really well," he says. "Best ever."

I look down at the money in my hand. Part of me wants to give it back. But I don't. It goes straight in my pocket.

Worry Book

Seriously, though. Where did he get it?

CHAPTER 26

It's only been a day since Tel put all those stickers up, and we've already had a few messages. None of them are to do with Ronnie, which Tel isn't happy about, but it's still early days.

We went out investigating who kicked the heads off Mr Gilbert's flowers last night, but there wasn't much we could do. It's not like we can dust for footprints or whatever.

My phone pings with a new message through the website. Here we go. Is this a Ronnie lead?

Morning, guys. This is a little embarrassing, but I need your help. I'm trapped inside my house. By a swan. Every time I try to leave, it chases me back inside. I've called the police,

but they say they're too busy to come out any
time soon. The animal welfare people are too
far away, as well. Thing is, I really need to get
to work in time for the start of my shift at ten.
If I don't, I might get fired. Can you help?

Bradley (102 Ivatt Road)

Now, this is going to be tricky. Every other time I've been out as Moon Boy, it's been late at night. Now I'm going to have to break cover in broad daylight. I fold up the costume as small as I can and stuff it into a bag.

"Where are you off to this early?" says Mum.

"Just going to see my friend," I say.

"He's being all secretive lately," says Dad, in one of his good moods. "I reckon he's got himself a little girlfriend."

"Have not," I snap.

Dad chuckles and ruffles my hair. "What's in the bag, son? A bunch of roses and some Milk Tray?"

I keep walking, heading straight for the door. "Nope. See you later!"

There's a block of public toilets at the end of the precinct, so I head in there to change. Man, it stinks.

I try and hold my breath, but it takes too long to get the costume on, and I'll die if I don't breathe in the foul, poop-tainted air.

When I come out of the cubicle, a bloke is on his way in and nearly has a heart attack when he sees me.

"Are you one of those superheroes?" he asks.

I just nod.

"Bit of a stupid question, that, wasn't it?" he says.

I nod again.

Star Kid is waiting for me at the top of Ivatt Road, hands on his hips, all business.

"Morning," he says.

"I feel kind of stupid," I say.

He nods. "These costumes are a little less intimidating in daylight, aren't they? We'd better press on."

We follow the cycle path to 102. I notice, with a shudder, that it's over the way from Bloody Mary's house.

"Is it true what they say about her?" I ask Star Kid.

He shrugs. "Probably not, but do you fancy going over and finding out?"

As I stare, I see a shape shambling past the window

and quickly look away. I don't want Bloody Mary to see me, even if I am in costume.

There's a bloke hanging out of the kitchen window of 102. He's a heavy-metal type: long beard and pierced nose.

"All right, lads?" he says. "I'm Bradley."

"I can't see the swan," Star Kid growls.

"Yeah, it lulls you into a false sense of security like that," says Bradley. "Watch this."

He leaves the window and comes to the front door. As soon as it opens, the swan – a white blur of fury – comes charging from around the side of the house. Bradley quickly slams the door, then goes back to his window. "See? I'm a prisoner in my own house!"

Star Kid puffs out his cheeks. "OK. Well, let's try and help you out then, shall we? Come on, Moon Boy."

We creep across the lawn towards the swan. It sees us coming and its feathers go up.

"That is one racked-off bird," I say.

We take another step and it hisses at us. Star Kid screeches to a halt. His eyes are wide, horrified.

"Everything all right?"

"Fine," he says. "I just didn't know they could, you know, hiss like that."

"So how are we going to do this?" I say.

Star Kid takes a little torch off his belt and flashes it on and off. The swan just stares at him like he's showing it a card trick.

"I don't think it knows Morse code," I say.

"Well, do you have any better ideas?" he snaps. His Star Kid voice is mostly gone by now.

I pull out my phone and skim-read an article called "How to handle an angry swan".

"It says here they can break your arm," I say.

"What?" Star Kid says.

I shrug. "It also says to try and catch hold of its neck first. Fancy a go?"

Star Kid takes a deep breath, then gingerly puts his hand out. The swan seems to take that as a personal insult and tries to peck him.

"How did this thing even get here?" Star Kid growls at Bradley.

"Beats me," says Bradley. "It's not as if we've even got any canals around here. It just appeared in my front garden this morning."

Star Kid takes a step back. I put my hand on his shoulder. "You're not scared of swans are you, Star Kid?"

"No," he says. "I'm just *wary*, that's all."

I take a step to the right and the swan follows

me. "How about this?" I whisper to Star Kid. I don't know why I'm whispering. It's not as if the swan can understand me. "I distract it, you grab it."

"Hang on just a second, why do I have to grab it?" says Star Kid.

"You've got the upper body strength from doing the fighting thingy," I say. "Don't worry, I'll shout out the instructions."

I hop up and down, thrashing my arms around. "Come on, swanny swanny! Come here! There's a good bird!"

The swan advances on me, its long neck extended and its beak open.

"OK," I say to Star Kid. "You need to go for the neck. Nice, strong grip."

Star Kid lunges for the swan and grabs its neck. The swan does not take kindly to this, hissing and furiously flapping its wings like we're about to bung it in the oven for Sunday dinner.

"What do I do now?" Star Kid shrieks.

"It says to hold it like a banjo!" I yell.

"Do I look like the kind of person that's ever held a banjo?" he screams. "What does that mean?"

"Grab its body!"

Star Kid tries to hold the swan's body with his

spare arm, but it's flapping too hard and he has to let go completely. The swan is enraged now and is furiously charging at us down the cycle path.

"Retreat!" Star Kid yells as we run.

The swan hisses and honks as it builds up speed. Ahead, a man rounds the corner, hands jammed into his pockets. Oh no. Is that...?

"BANG!" he goes.

The swan skids to a halt, then turns around, runs the other way and takes off.

Bradley runs past us, waving. "Thanks, lads. I'll recommend you to all my mates!"

When I turn around, Ronnie is smiling at us. Star Kid glares at him, fists clenched. Ronnie's smile is warm and friendly, but there's something else just behind it, barely hidden from view.

"Hello, lads!" he says. "Fancy seeing you here!"

Star Kid stays silent, so I do too.

"I've been looking high and low for you," he goes on. "I was about to send a message to that website of yours. Very professional, by the way."

"What do you want?" says Star Kid, his superhero voice still there, but wobbly.

Ronnie chuckles. "Just to congratulate you on a job well done. It's a wonderful thing you're doing."

He pulls a hand out of his pocket and I see he's clutching a wedge of notes. Just like Dad did the other day. He holds it out to us.

"Here you go," he says. "Buy yourselves some new utility belts, or something."

"We don't want your money," says Star Kid. "You can't buy us like you've bought everything else around here."

For a split second, that friendly smile disappears and I see a glimpse of what's underneath. I have to look away. But as quickly as it vanished, it's back.

"Fair enough," says Ronnie, jamming the money back into his pocket. "You have principles. I respect that."

It goes quiet again. We just stand there, facing him, even though every instinct in my body is screaming at me to run.

Ronnie cocks his head to one side. "I know who you are, kid. Don't think I haven't seen you following me around the place."

Star Kid says nothing, just clenches his jaw.

"You probably think I have something to do with what happened all those years ago, but I'll say it again: I don't. That was nothing to do with me."

Hang on, what's he talking about?

"So if that's your angle," says Ronnie, "you can forget it. Am I making myself clear?"

"Will that be all?" says Star Kid.

Ronnie turns his gaze on me for the first time. It's like he's trying to see through my mask. He stares long, hard, stone-faced. I can't look him in the eye. It's like looking at the sun. I stare at the tip of his shoulder.

"Yeah," he says, finally. "That'll be all. For now."

And with that, he pushes past us down the cycle path.

Star Kid turns and watches him go. He's shaking.

"Are you OK?" I ask him.

"I'm fine," he says.

Ronnie takes a left and disappears into the estate.

"What did he mean when he said about the thing that happened years ago?" I ask.

Star Kid looks at me. "Oh," he says. "Long story."

It doesn't look like he's going to say more than that.

Worry Book

How long could this story be?

CHAPTER 27

I keep googling Ronnie, but there's hardly anything about him. There's one news story from ages ago where he paid for a bench to be put up in the precinct. He's referred to as "local businessman Ronald Reynolds". There's a photo of him shaking hands with someone from the council. That's all.

I don't know what I was expecting, really. It's not as if master criminals have their own websites, is it? Their whole thing is that they keep themselves hidden away. I think that's why our old house was behind a gate. It kept the rest of the world from coming around and snooping in Dad's business.

I close the laptop and stare at the Wall Bears. Mum and Millie have not long left for work and day care and now I'm bored. I get up and go to the fridge.

I'm not hungry – in fact, I only had breakfast about fifteen minutes ago – but I'm still looking. Maybe I think I can find something to do in there? Like, if I keep looking, eventually it'll spit out a new PS5 game?

I want to message Tel and see if he's up for doing something, but I won't. I really like hanging out with him, but we already spend a lot of time together and I don't want to seem too keen. I remember when my old mate Will got a girlfriend and he texted her so much she dumped him for being too clingy. I don't want Tel to dump me, I guess is what I'm saying.

Hmm. That's weird. There's a notepad on the table. A small, blue one with white plastic rings at the top. I've never seen it before. I grab one of those little fruit drinks Mum buys for Millie that I secretly quite like and go over to the table to take a look. This is how bored I am. I'm opening notepads in search of entertainment. I remember reading a story when I was in primary school, about a kid who opened a mysterious book and it transported him and his mates to pirate times. I wonder how I'd be as a pirate? Probably about as good as I am as a superhero.

I pick up the notepad and am about to look inside when the front door opens.

"Oh," says Dad. "I thought you'd be out."

He should be in work by now, shouldn't he?

"Think I'm staying in today," I say. But he's not listening. I can tell. He's looking at the notepad in my hand.

"I forgot that," he says, holding his hand out for it. "Need it for work."

I hand it over and Dad quickly sticks it in his pocket. He stares at me for a second. "Right. Better get going. I'm running late as it is." And with that, he turns around and heads back out.

Weird.

My phone buzzes. It's Mum calling. What now? Has she got a secret notepad she can't do without, too?

"Hello?"

"Finn! Finley! Is that what it's short for? Shark Finn? Salt and Finegar?"

"Is everything all right, Gino?" I say, cutting him off before he lists another eight hundred Finn jokes.

"You're a young man, aren't you?" he says. "A young, strong man?"

"Um, maybe?"

"Good, well, I'm going to need your help with something. I've got a big breakfast order that's come in and I need someone to deliver it. Paid work, of course."

Hmm. Money. Wouldn't mind a bit of that. Might be able to get out and actually do stuff.

"OK," I say.

"You're a lifesaver," says Gino. "Because this isn't a customer I want to keep waiting if I can help it. Be here in fifteen."

Ah, well. At least it'll give me something to do. I put the weirdness of Dad's notepad to the back of my mind and get ready.

When I walk into Gino's, Mum is chatting to a couple of old ladies at a table. She looks different when she's here. I don't think it's just the apron, either; it's something else. I can't figure it out.

"Ohhhh!" Gino comes out of the kitchen with a tea towel over his shoulder and a hairnet on. One of the ladies Mum is talking to wolf whistles at him.

"Here he is," says Gino, pointing at me. "The man of the hour. Are you feeling strong, my friend?"

"I suppose so," I say.

"He supposes so," says Gino to Mum. "All right, it's in the back. I'll show you where."

Gino leads me to the kitchen and a box of wrapped sandwiches and polystyrene boxes. "Here it is," he says. "Now, why don't you be a superhero and take it over there for me?"

I don't register it to begin with, but then I see the amused look on his face. "What?" I say.

Gino laughs. "Come on," he whispers. "I might be getting old, but I'm not about to forget the exact same mask on this superhero everyone's talking about dropping into my herb garden, am I? And the other one is that boy from Primrose House; what's his name, Tel?"

I say nothing. Even though he has completely figured it out, I'm not going to admit it. Gino grabs my shoulder and squeezes it.

"Look, I get that you're not going to admit anything to me – superhero code and all that – but just be careful, OK? Your mother's got enough to worry about without you getting hurt."

What am I supposed to say? "Don't know what you're talking about," I mumble.

"Course you don't," he says. "Anyway, this stuff is hot off the grill, so I need it over there pronto." He taps the side of the box.

"Where is it going?" I ask.

Gino chuckles. "Silly me. This is for Ronnie Reynolds."

He must clock my reaction, because he smiles wider. "I've got a feeling you know where he lives already, right?"

"Maybe."

"Looks like he's having a breakfast meeting today with some other like-minded citizens. Like I said, be careful." He winks and goes to walk away.

"Hold on," I say. "Does he have to give me money, or…"

Gino laughs again, but this time it's a hollow, cold laugh. "Ronnie doesn't pay, Finn. Ronnie never pays. Now go on, faster than a speeding bullet, OK?"

I pick up the box and head out of the door. I wait until I'm out of sight before resting it on the wall and calling Tel.

"What are you so excited about?" he says.

"I've got his sandwiches," I say. "I'VE GOT HIS SANDWICHES!"

"Am I speaking to a seagull?"

I stop for a second and try to get a grip. "Ronnie," I say. "I have his order from Gino's. I have to deliver it right now."

"Right now?"

"Right now," I say.

"Oh, my, oh, my, oh, my," he says. "OK, bring it here as quick as you can. I'll think of something."

I check over my shoulder to see if I'm being watched, before picking the box back up and heading to Tel's.

After having to nudge the main door open with my foot and nearly dropping the whole thing, I reach Tel's flat, where he throws the door open before I can even knock. He's wearing burgundy button-down pyjamas and slippers.

"Nice PJs," I say.

"Never mind that," he snaps. "Look at this."

He shows me an apple-sized ornament. "It's the Colosseum in Rome. My uncle brought it back for us. At the time I was like, 'Really? A tacky ornament?' But now I could kiss the tight-fisted old swine." He looks doubtful for a second. "This is the type of thing an Italian bistro would give away as a free gift, right?"

"I suppose so," I say.

Tel turns the ornament over and lifts a black plastic lid off the top, revealing the bugging device inside. "It's the best I could do on short notice," he says.

His eyes rest on the box. He seems to be thinking about something, but he quickly shakes his head and puts the ornament in, nestling it between two containers.

"All right, go! I'll get everything set up this end. Get back here as quick as you can."

I hurry down the stairs and across the car park,

my heart thudding in my ears. As I walk, I try and rearrange the containers so the Colosseum is more hidden, but there's only so much I can do. I start rehearsing my lines in my head.

Hi! Delivery from Gino's.

Should I say hi? Will they laugh? How about hello? Too formal. I feel like I'm back at Dad's old pub, Uncle Shane finding pound coins behind my ear and ruffling my hair too hard. I'd always second-guess myself, questioning everything about what I was doing. Should I sit with my knees apart like Dad? How about my face? Am I doing the right thing with my face?

My brain whirs so fast that seeing Ronnie's house ahead almost takes me by surprise. The grey blinds in the downstairs windows are pulled tightly shut and the only signs of life come from a thin strip of light seeping under the door.

I ring the doorbell, which reminds me of the one we had on our gate back at the old house. It has a camera and a little speaker. I remember Dad used to look at the feed on his phone and tell charity workers to go away. But not in those words.

"Hello?" a voice crackles through the speaker.

"Good morning!" I say. "Gelivery from Dino's."

I screw my eyes shut. What an idiot.

"About time."

The door opens and Ronnie stands there. Without a word, he holds out his hands and I pass him the box.

"There's a, there's a, there's a free gift inside," I blurt out.

Oh, why did you have to draw attention to it, sludgebrain?

Ronnie puts the box down on a sideboard and shrugs. "That to make up for it being late?"

"Y-yes," I say. "That's what it is. Anyway, enjoy your breakfast."

"Hang about, kid," he says. He reaches into the back pocket of his jeans and passes me twenty pounds. "For your trouble."

"Oh," I say. "Th-thanks."

Ronnie says nothing else, just shuts the door. I cram the money into my pocket and walk as quickly as I can back to Tel's. I don't want to run in case anyone sees me and suspects something.

When I get there, I find Tel hunched over the computer in his bedroom. On the screen, thin green lines snake up and down as sounds from the breakfast meeting drift through the speakers.

"Got anything so far?" I ask.

"Just a load of gross mouth noises at the moment," he replies. "It sounds like they've left the ornament in the box rather than throw it away, so that's something."

"Right, let's get on with it." I hear a voice which sounds like Ronnie's. "Freddie, how you doing this week?"

"Best week in a while, boss," this other voice says. "Staked out some new territory over in Gatesford. Took the new boy out with me, showed him the ropes."

"Yeah? How did he do?" asked Ronnie.

"Like a duck to water," said the other bloke.

"That's what I like to hear," says Ronnie. "How about you, Mal?"

"Pretty good," he says. "That new restaurant that opened in town, the Chinese? Got them paying me two hundred a week."

Tel shoots me a look. "There it is!" he whispers. "Evidence of extortion!"

I shake my head. "Not enough," I say. "He'll just say he got a job there, or something. We need to catch them saying something more incriminating."

I catch Tel's eyes lingering on me again, but I ignore him and focus on the screen. I remember overhearing Dad saying things like that, boasting in the pub about how he wriggled out of trouble with the police.

We sit and listen to the whole meeting, but there's nothing juicy enough to get them on. It's all too vague.

The sound gets louder and the speakers squeal. "What do you want doing with this, Ronnie?" someone asks.

Oh no, he's talking about the Colosseum, isn't he?

"Just stick it on the side," he says. "My wife likes tat like that."

Tel slaps his hand across his chest. "Thanks, Mrs Ronnie," he whispers.

All the men leave, and it sounds like Ronnie has moved to another part of the house.

"What now?" I ask.

"We wait," says Tel. "That bug should have a twenty-four hour battery life. He has to say something during that time. Surely."

CHAPTER 28

Well, we waited for another four hours and he said nothing. Zilch. I had to head home, but Tel said he would listen all day and all night if he had to.

It's eight in the morning now, and I bet he hasn't left his computer. I dread to think what he did when he needed the toilet. Still, I'm kind of jealous I'm not there listening, because right now, in our flat, it's Argument Time!

Wow. It must have been, what, two days since the last one? That's got to be a new record, especially since moving here.

It's money again. I can't tell exactly what it is about money, because me and Millie are lying on her bed, sharing my earphones again. We've got our routine down to a T now.

Millie is falling asleep with her thumb in her mouth, so I grab the laptop and check the website for new messages.

Dear Superheroes,

I'd like to report Tom Jeffries for being a wasteman.

Yours Sincerely,

E. Norma Sbum

Our first prank message. Have to admit, I laughed.

The argument seems to be dying down now, moving on to phase two: the angry silence. That phase is a doozy. Dad has stretched that one out for days before. The worst was when they had the argument about whether we were going to do what the police wanted us to do. Mum wanted to go along with it. Dad wanted to go on the run, like Uncle Shane. Mum won in the end, but he didn't like it one bit.

I carefully pull my arm from underneath Millie's head and ease myself on to the floor, centimetre by centimetre. It's only then that I see something on my desk. It's her Santa toy, the one Tel gave her. And underneath is a note. It says:

To Santa,
I want too go home.
Luv,
Millie

I close my eyes and try to swallow the cricket-ball-sized lump in my throat. Oh, Mils, I wish Santa could sort that for you, I really do. But I think that might be too big an ask, even for him.

My phone buzzes and I snatch it up before it wakes Millie.

"Phineas, we need to talk," says Tel, skipping all the pleasantries.

"Is it about E. Norma Sbum?" I ask.

"What are you on about?" he snaps. "It's about Ronnie. I've been listening all night and he's been saying NOTHING. It's like bugging a mime's house."

"So what's the plan?" I ask.

"The plan is we're finished if he doesn't say anything incriminating within the next two hours. That's how much battery life the bug has left."

"Oh," I say.

"Oh, indeed," says Tel. "And I don't think he's suddenly going to launch into a song and dance routine of all the bad things he's done, like some kind of Disney villain, any time soon, so we need to have a rethink."

I get up and move a little further away from Millie. Tel is so loud and riled up, I'm worried he'll wake her up.

"Why don't I like the sound of that?" I say.

"Look, it's fine," says Tel, sounding like someone who's about to suggest going bungee jumping without a rope. "All we have to do is engage him in conversation."

"And how are we going to do that?"

"I've thought about it" – he hesitates and I can hear the hum of the Colosseum feed in the background – "and we need to meet with him. Well, I say 'we'."

"Right," I say. "So you're going on your own?"

Tel laughs. "I can't go! He knows who I am! This is a job for Moon Boy."

I stand up, sit back down and stand up again. "You want me to go inside his *house*? On my own?"

"Not you, Phineas. *Moon Boy*," says Tel. "I was quite clear about that."

I pace up and down my room. Three paces from

end to end. I look out of the window, but all I see is the landing.

"But I ... I..."

"You *can*," says Tel, accurately predicting the next word I was going to say. "This is incredibly important to me. You know it is. This could be our only opportunity to get him. If we don't even try, how can we look at ourselves in the mirror? You heard them in that meeting. If we take them down, we're going to lift so many people out of misery."

"But ... but..."

"You can do it, Moon Boy," he says. "I know you. I know you better than you think I do, because you're like me. You've spent your whole life having people tell you you're not good enough because you're not like them."

I swallow. He's right. For him, it was school bullies. For me, it's my dad.

"You look at people like Ronnie and think you don't measure up, but you do, Moon Boy, you do."

"Stop, Tel," I say. "Just stop. I'll do it."

203

CHAPTER 29

I'm back at Ronnie's front door, but this time I'm in costume. Tel has told me everything I have to say. It's almost as if he was planning it for hours.

My finger hovers over the doorbell. I only have an hour before the battery dies, but I can't bring myself to press it. *Come on. You heard what Tel said. You can do this. You are going to press that button in ten … nine … eight … seven … six…*

The door opens and Ronnie stands there, a sly smirk on his face. "Bit early for trick-or-treaters, isn't it?" he says.

"H-hello," I say. "I was thinking about what you said to us the other day and I, um, I want to take you up on it."

Ronnie frowns at me with his bulging arms

folded. I feel like I'm being studied. "Where's your mate?"

"He doesn't know I'm here."

Ronnie chuckles. "Doesn't surprise me. I don't think he likes me very much." He jerks his head backwards. "Come on in."

I follow him inside the house. Stay calm, Damian. FINN! Finn. MOON BOY! Stay calm, Moon Boy. Tel can hear everything that's happening. You're not going to get murdered.

Inside, it reminds me of our old house. The walls are all plain white, with framed paintings of squiggles in grey and black. The seats are all black leather and the TV is like something you'd find in a cinema.

"Can I get you anything ... what's your name, anyway?"

"It's Moon Boy," I say.

Ronnie throws his head back and laughs, and I catch a glimpse of his gold fillings. "Nice. Very mysterious. It does make you sound like you go around showing people your rear end, though."

Oh. It kind of does, doesn't it? Ah well I'll worry about that later.

"So, can I get you anything? You don't look old enough for a beer. How old are you, anyway?"

Don't give him any personal information, Moon Boy. Don't give him anything he can use against you. He's a very clever man.

"I can't tell you that," I say.

Ronnie walks over to a chair and sits down. He motions for me to sit on the couch. When I do, I regret it. Rubber on leather sounds horrible. It's like I'm constantly farting. On the mantelpiece, next to a framed photo of an old lady who must be Ronnie's mum, I see the Colosseum. *Don't keep staring at it. Just pretend it's not there.*

"So what can I do for you, Moon Boy?" he says.

I shift in my seat, which lets another ripper go free.

"I'm getting sick of Star Kid," I say. "His obsession with you is getting too much."

"You're telling me," says Ronnie. "I caught the little bleeder going through my bins, once."

Why, Tel? Why?

"Yeah," I say. "Well, this is it. I've seen you around the estate, and I've seen you've got a nice house, and this superhero gig is all right and everything, but it doesn't exactly pay."

Ronnie raises an eyebrow. Sitting there, he reminds me of a lion, looking over his territory: relaxed, but ready to pounce any second. There's a silence, and I can tell I'm going to have to be the one to fill it.

"So, I guess I was wondering if I could, you know, work for you?"

Ronnie sits back and crosses his legs. "Interesting. I've never had a kid in a fancy dress costume on my payroll before."

"I'm a really hard worker," I say. "And I'm a fast learner, too."

Ronnie holds up his hands. "Spare me the CV. I started in the business when I was your age, too. Running errands for Jackie Jones. He was a tough man, was Jackie. But he was fair. And I try to be fair, too, Moon Boy. And normally, someone coming to see me like this, showing initiative, I'd offer them a trial run. But not this time."

"Oh," I say. "Why not?"

He looks at me like I'm an idiot. "You're wearing a mask, kid. I haven't a clue who you are. Do you really think I'm going to send you around making pick-ups looking like that? People will think I've gone barmy!"

I thought this might come up. Well, Tel thought it might come up. That's why he told me what to say.

"'I'm just being careful. I won't take it off until I'm

sure we're both serious," I say. "So when you say pick-ups, what do you mean, exactly?"

Ronnie rubs his chin and leans forward. "I'm going to need you to take that mask off before I answer any more questions."

Ah. We didn't prepare for this. Why didn't we prepare for this?

"W-what if I don't?"

Ronnie shrugs. "Doesn't bother me. You and your mate can carry on doing what you're doing. Busting muggers and shoplifters is a good thing, in my book. But when you start interfering in my business? That's when we've got a problem."

I swallow hard. I want to say the main reason people are mugging and shoplifting is him, but I can't. And it makes me think about what Dad used to do and everything that he must have caused.

"OK," I say. "So if I take the mask off, you'll give me a chance?"

"Sure," says Ronnie. "On a trial basis, of course."

I glance over at the Colosseum and imagine Tel on the other end, hunched over his computer, screaming instructions at me that I can't hear. What would he be saying?

I reach behind my head and unzip the mask. I

hesitate before lifting it off. I wish I had an earpiece in with Tel giving me instructions. That would make this so much easier.

"What are you so interested in over there?" Ronnie jolts me out of my thoughts, mask still on.

"Over where?"

"The mantelpiece," he says.

Oh no. *Have I been staring at the Colosseum the entire time?*

"Nothing," I say.

"You keep looking over there," he says. "What is it?"

Now I can picture Tel screaming so loud the neighbours are hammering on the walls.

"Oh," I say again. "Just that ... photo."

Ronnie turns and looks, then snaps his focus back to me. "That's my mum," he says.

I clear my throat. "It's just a nice photo," I say. "Good ... what's the word? Composition?"

He stares at me. And stares. And stares. I shift in my seat, so the only sound in the room very much resembles a fart.

"So shall I take my mask off, then?"

Ronnie sits back in his chair. "Go ahead."

I pull the mask off and put it in my lap. Ronnie

doesn't react. I look at the rug. I figure it's the only way to stop my eyes drifting over to the Colosseum.

"All right," he says. "Now isn't that better? No need for any masks."

I nod a little, but right now I feel more exposed than I ever have before. It's like one of those dreams where I show up to school naked.

"What's your name?" he says.

"Damian," I say, blurting it out before I have a second to think about it. "My name's Damian."

Ronnie seems to find this funny. "Perfect," he laughs.

I'm used to that: the whole devil thing. I think that's why Dad picked the name. I was happy when I got the chance to get rid of it.

"So here's what you're going to do, Damian," says Ronnie, "because I'm not a hundred per cent sure you're for real yet. You're going to accompany one of my men on a collection. He's new, but he's proven he can be trusted. I think the two of you will get along nicely. If all that goes well, I'll let you do some collections on your own. Nothing dangerous; low-risk drops. Give it a few weeks, and you could be earning a nice bit of money."

For a second, it's like my brain flicks to a different

mode. From light to dark. I could use some money, after all. The whole family could. If I am really good at this, I could make enough for us to move somewhere nicer...

But the Colosseum on the shelf seems to be screaming at me, reminding me of my mission.

"What kind of drops are they?" I ask. "Like, who are we collecting from?"

"Businesses, mainly," he says. "They pay us for our services."

I swallow hard. I remember hearing that Dad and Uncle Shane used to be involved in that kind of thing. I secretly read about it online during the court case. I wish I hadn't.

"What services?" I say.

Ronnie chuckles. "Inquisitive young man, aren't you? If you were going for a job at McDonalds, would you demand to know what's in the burgers?"

I shrug, desperately clinging to my nerve like it's a cliff edge. "I think it's fair to know what kind of business I'm working for."

Ronnie gets up and stands over me, before slowly walking over to the mantelpiece and picking up a long, black fire poker. He holds it up to the light like he's inspecting it, before bringing it down to rest on his open palm. I try not to freak out and imagine what he might do with it. I'm a superhero. I'm supposed to be brave.

"We offer protection for businesses," he says. "They pay us a fair weekly or monthly fee, and we make sure no harm comes to their premises. We do what you do, really, except we don't wear silly costumes, and we're smart enough to charge."

No way. We're nothing like him. I know him. I feel like I've known him all my life. The only thing that money buys protection from is him. But the important thing is, he's talking. We've got him. But it's not enough. We need more.

"What happens if they don't pay?" I ask.

Ronnie steps closer to me, gently patting his palm with the poker. "That will be covered in your training. I've already said too much."

"What do you mean?" I ask.

"I'm a very careful man, Damian. I prefer to let my employees do most of the talking. As I say, the fella who's training you will show you the ropes."

I can't help but glance at the Colosseum again. We've probably got ten minutes at the most before it dies.

"OK, but I kind of need more info," I say. "Got to decide if the job is right for me."

Ronnie's hand tightens around the end of the poker. He doesn't speak. He's sizing me up again, but this time he's taking it more seriously.

"I've seen you before," he says.

I gulp. "Well, I do live on the estate."

"No, no, no, not that." He points at me with the poker. "You've been here before."

"No, I haven't!" I say.

It's no good. He remembers. Of course he does.

"You delivered our breakfasts from Gino's yesterday morning."

"OK, I did," I say. "I told you, I'm a hard worker."

But he's not listening. He's marching over to the mantelpiece and picking up the Colosseum.

"Thought you'd bring me a little gift, did you?" he growls, ripping off the flimsy plastic lid and pulling out the bug.

I run for the door, but it's locked and there's no key and he's got me, he's got me, he's got me.

CHAPTER 30

I can't breathe. How am I supposed to answer him when I can't breathe? He's pressing me into the wall with his arm and belly and his disgusting breath is blasting my face.

"Where is that hooked up to? Is it recording? Tell me!"

But I can't breathe, even to beg him to stop.

"It's that other kid, isn't it?" Ronnie growls.

He grips the back of my head and throws me down the hall. I try to jump up and run, but it's like my chest is being gripped in a vice and I fall over again.

Then I'm being lifted off the ground. I fight and struggle, but I have no choice. Ronnie opens a door and carries me down some stairs. It's dark down here.

When I hit the floor, a sharp pain shoots up my

leg. I must have gone over on my ankle. My eyes fill with tears.

"Look at you," Ronnie sneers. "You're pathetic."

He's just Dad, I tell myself. This is just like dealing with Dad. You can do this. I try and put my foot down, but the pain surges back and now the tears are running down my face.

"Not so much of a superhero now, are you?" he says. "Crying like a pathetic baby."

I run my hand down my face, but it does nothing to stop the tears.

"Now you're going to tell me where that recording is."

The only light is coming from a small window above his head. No one would hear me down here even if I screamed.

"What if I don't?" I say.

"Doesn't matter," he says. "Because I'll find out anyway. But if you tell me now, it'll make life much less painful for both of us."

"Look, I don't know, OK?" I say. "He won't tell me where he lives. It's the superhero code."

I know it's ridiculous, but I'm desperate, and his laugh suggests he's not buying it.

"Pull the other one, kid," he says. "You know

exactly where he lives, but like I say, it doesn't matter. Because all I have to do is make a call and my boys will find out where he is in five minutes. And as soon as they've destroyed the recording, I'm going to send them to that little café to have a word with the owner."

"But Gino didn't have anything to do with it!" I say.

"Of course he didn't," says Ronnie sarcastically. "That fool has been disrespecting me for years. He was in on it all along."

"Please don't," I say. "My mum works there."

A look goes across Ronnie's face. It's too dark to tell what it is, but something has changed.

"Your mum?"

"Yeah."

He looks like he's confused about something. I don't know what. I'm about to take advantage and make a run for the stairs when—

SMASSSSSHHHHHHHH!

It sounds like something huge has crashed through a window somewhere above us. Ronnie takes off upstairs to investigate. I let him go a little way ahead, then follow. It may be my only chance to escape.

When I get to the top of the stairs, Ronnie is

bombing into the lounge, where something is tussling with the blinds.

"Have you got a death wish, or something?" he roars at the shape, flailing to free itself.

With a big push, the shape launches itself out, bringing the blinds, rail and chunks of plaster with it. I'm about to make a run for the door when the figure flips over and jumps to its feet.

"Surrender!" Star Kid yells.

CHAPTER 31

Star Kid seems to anticipate Ronnie's swing and ducks just in time, sending Ronnie stumbling into the wreckage on the floor. He manages to stay upright and rounds on us again.

"Moon Boy! Assume the position!"

I remember this from our first training session. I go down on all fours. Star Kid advances on him, clutching a jagged piece of plaster. Ronnie backs up and falls over me, landing heavily on the ground. Star Kid pulls me to my feet, scoops my mask up off the sofa and hands it to me.

"Proper uniform, Moon Boy, proper uniform."

He smiles and nods, before turning and running to the hole where the window used to be and leaping through. I'm right behind him like a shot.

Ronnie crashes through after us, screaming and howling.

"Where are we going?" I shout over the noise.

"Just keep running!" Star Kid shouts back, which I do, trying to ignore the pain in my leg.

"I'll kill you!" Ronnie screams, huffing and puffing behind us.

When we reach the precinct, Star Kid stops and faces Ronnie.

"What are you doing?" I hiss.

Star Kid doesn't answer, just stands and stares at the exhausted Ronnie stumbling past the community centre. He stands in front of us, sweat pouring down his face.

"Tell me where the recording is," he says, barely able to get his words out.

"Nah," says Star Kid.

Ronnie staggers closer to us, but has to stop and rest with his hands on his knees.

"Pathetic," says Star Kid.

He looks up at us and opens his mouth as if he's going to say something, but realizes it would take up too much energy.

Through the corner of my eye, I see the café door open and Gino standing in the doorway. Then I see

Ali come and stand outside his shop, and George from the chippy comes out to see what's going on.

"You're done, Ronnie," says Star Kid.

Ronnie straightens up and winces. "You don't know what you're talking about. I'm going nowhere. And you aren't getting away with this. None of you!"

He starts walking closer to us, his chest rising and falling rapidly.

"Stand your ground, Moon Boy," Star Kid says to me through the side of his mouth.

I sense a figure approaching from the side, then another, then another. It's Gino, Ali and George. They stand in front of us, arms folded.

"What do you think you're doing?" Ronnie almost screams. "Are you forgetting who runs this place?"

"You never ran this place," Pat says, coming out of the community centre and joining the line. "You're a leech on it. I spend every day of my life in there" – she points at the door – "trying to put right what you do wrong."

Ronnie ignores her and jabs his finger in Gino's face. "I know what you did."

"What did I do, Ronnie?" he says.

I see Mum come to the café door and I step back slightly, so Star Kid will be blocking her view of me.

"Bugging me!" he screeches. "Sending that ornament with a microphone in it."

Gino turns around and raises an eyebrow at me, before turning back to Ronnie and laughing. "I think the pressure's getting to you, Ronald. You're paranoid."

"The estate has had enough of you," says Star Kid. "Your threats mean nothing."

Ronnie laughs, a high, hysterical cackle. "You'll see! You just wait."

A whoop cuts through the noise and Ronnie's confused face is lit with flashes of blue.

"Like I say, Ronnie," says Star Kid. "It's over."

CHAPTER 32

"A crime boss who has terrorized a Tammerstone estate for over a decade has finally been brought to justice. By superheroes. Gary Duffy has more."

"Ronald Reynolds was said to rule the Ampleforth Estate with an iron fist, forcing local businesses to pay protection money and lending money to residents at extortionate rates of interest. Police tried and failed to pin him down for years. Until now. Enter Star Kid and Moon Boy."

I hug the sofa cushion tight and adjust my bad leg, which is resting on a pouffe. I told them I did it tripping down some steps. Dad is sitting next to me, watching the TV, stone-faced. Mum stands in the kitchen doorway, watching as she dries a plate, while Millie sits on the floor drawing pictures of dogs.

Star Kid appears on screen. I refused. We had a bit of an argument about it, but I wouldn't budge. I don't care if I'm wearing a mask; I can't risk it.

"We managed to place a bugging device in his home. My sidekick – that's right, *sidekick* – Moon Boy then went to his house and nudged him into incriminating himself. Problem is, Ronnie rumbled Moon Boy, so I had to rush around and smash his window in with a wheelbarrow to rescue him."

The reporter goes on: "Following Reynolds' arrest for a public order offence, police listened to the recording and conducted a raid, where evidence was seized and several of his associates were also arrested."

"I'm glad he's gone," says Mum. "Gino was telling me all about him."

Dad turns up the TV and ignores her.

"This place is going to change overnight." Now Pat is on. "In my work at the food bank, I would see so many people driven to desperation by that man. That's not going to happen any more, and I couldn't be happier. Those two young men have done this community a world of good."

Dad grunts and changes the channel. He doesn't

have to say anything. I know how he feels about superheroes.

It's been a couple of days since the arrest. Tel and I haven't met face to face since then. He said it'd be better if we laid low for a few days, just in case there were some of Ronnie's men left over, looking for us. The news that a load of them have been arrested has put my mind at rest. At least a little bit.

We've been getting loads of supportive messages through the website, and now we're on the local news, even more are coming in. It's really nice, but I still feel weird. In movies and comics, when the big bad villain is defeated, everyone is super happy and it's the best day of their lives, but I don't feel like that. I'm still on edge, like Ronnie could walk in at any moment. Or Uncle Shane.

My phone buzzes, which makes me jump a little. It's a message from Tel. I get up and read it in the bedroom. I can't risk Dad seeing it over my shoulder.

Seen that message?

Which one, Phineas? We've got like 50.

The dog one.

I go to the inbox and scroll through. Then I see it: *LOST DOG.*

You think it's legit?

Yes. I know the family who sent it. What's the matter? Do you think bad guys are trying to entrap us?

No. Just checking, that's all.

Worry Book

What if, though?

CHAPTER 33

Later that night, it's quite warm outside and I'm dressed up in rubber, hunting for a missing dog. I'd be lying if I said this was how I had imagined life would be on the Ampleforth Estate.

Here's the brief: the dog is a chihuahua called Tyson, and he's been missing since this morning. His owners, Mr and Mrs Garbett, are beside themselves with worry. Even though neither of us have any dog-finding experience, we are going to try our best.

We're standing at the top of Burley Close, not far from where he went missing. My leg is still a little sore, but I can walk on it without limping too badly now.

"Bit of a comedown, isn't it?" says Star Kid, hands on hips, surveying the area.

"They can't all be crime lord takedowns, I suppose," I say.

"True," says Star Kid. He digs the toe of his boot into the soil at the foot of an overgrown bush. "I suppose now he's gone it's going to be piffling stuff like missing dogs from here on out."

"Are you sad, in a way?" I ask him. "I mean, it's kind of like Batman without Joker. Now you've lost your reason to put on the costume."

"No," he says, firmly. "I'm not sad in the slightest. I'm glad he's gone."

Well, that told me.

I think I catch a glimpse of a dog zipping into the shadows behind some bins, but turns out it's just a cat. Ugh. Why are we looking for the tiniest dog in existence? You might as well send us out searching for a gerbil.

"And do you know something else?" Star Kid goes on. "The best thing about it was how everyone came together to get rid of him. He knew, in that moment, that we weren't going to stand for it any longer."

"I've been wondering about that," I say. "How come they didn't do it sooner?"

Star Kid starts off down the cycle path and I follow. We're lit up orange by the street lights above.

"Because they didn't know they could," he replies. "Neither did I. But something changed that day. It's like … you've seen the *Wizard of Oz*, haven't you? Tell me you've seen it."

"Yeah, my mum loves it."

"Good, because if you hadn't seen it, I'd have to re-evaluate some things. Anyway, what happened was exactly like that."

I think about it and try to find some kind of comparison. Was Ronnie wearing red slippers? Did he have flying monkeys working for him?

"How?" I say, giving up.

"Remember the bit where they go and see the wizard, and he's this huge, terrifying green head with fangs and fire all over the place?"

"Oh, yeah." I don't tell him I was so scared the first time I saw it I had nightmares and wet the bed. Dad screamed at me for that.

"And then Toto the dog pulls back the curtain and reveals that this big, scary entity is actually a sad old man creating a completely false illusion of power?" he goes on. "Well, all we did was pull back the curtain. Bang. People aren't afraid any more. We, my friend, were Toto."

I think back to that day. How he came puffing and

panting and red-faced, all alone, screaming empty threats at a couple of kids in superhero costumes. If I try to forget about how scared I was, I realize that he really did seem kind of sad.

There's no sign of Tyson on the other side of the underpass. It would be hard enough to spot him in daylight, let alone after eleven at night.

"This is hopeless," I say to Star Kid. "We're never going to find him."

Star Kid shakes his head like he's disappointed in me. "Never lose faith, Moon Boy. I never doubted for one second that I would get rid of Ronnie, and look what happened. Persistence pays off." He puts his fingers in his mouth and whistles. "Tyson! Here, boy!"

There's a bright light at the far end of the cycle path. To begin with, I think it's a bike, but it's bigger than that, more intense. And it can't be a motorbike because there's no engine noise. What is that thing?

"You see that?" I nudge Star Kid.

He squints at it as it approaches. It's moving pretty quick, bouncing up and down. As it gets closer, I see three figures behind it. As weird as it sounds, one of the silhouettes looks familiar. Oh. Oh no.

"Booyeah, booyeah, booyeah, booyeah!"

The light is coming from a TV camera. Beside the cameraman, there's another guy holding a big furry mic on a stick and with them, just as I suspected, it's Casey Kellman from *Awesome Kids*.

"BOOYEAH! I'm here in Tammerstone with Moon Boy and Star Kid, the superheroes who are protecting this part of the world so awesomely. YOU ARE … AWESOME KIDS!"

There's an awkward silence. Casey is grinning about three centimetres away from our faces, with big hair that poofs out from his head like an explosion.

"Actually, Casey," says Star Kid, breaking the deadlock. "It's Star Kid and Moon Boy. Not the other way around."

CHAPTER 34

"Just walk up the path and look natural!" Casey yells after us. "We want a nice heroic shot."

We walk towards the underpass together, the camera behind us.

"Did you do this?" I hiss through gritted teeth.

"Of course I didn't," says Star Kid. "What, you think I have Casey Kellman's phone number? You think I slid into his DMs? Surely you should have seen this coming? Bringing down Ronnie was always going to draw more attention."

"OK, guys, keep going!" Casey yells. "You're doing great!"

I'm really self-conscious about the way I walk now. I've never thought about it before, but now it's like I'm back at Dad's pub and I'm obsessing over whether I bend my knees enough.

"I need to go, Tel," I say.

He swats my arms. "Stop using my civilian name, you clod! And no way, you're not leaving me on my own again."

"But I can't be on TV," I say. "I just can't."

"I don't get this," says Star Kid. "Why not?"

I see a curtain open in a house to my right and someone peep out, probably wondering what the hell is going on.

"I've just never liked going on camera, that's all," I say.

"You guys look amazing!" Casey yells. "Work it!"

"You're aware you're wearing a mask, aren't you?"

"Yeah, I am, but..." I can see he's not going to let it go this time. "If I do this, will you do all the talking?"

"I don't know if I can manage that," he says. "I mean, you're always such a chatterbox when you're in that costume."

Casey applauds like he's just witnessed the best performance he's ever seen. "That was AWESOME! Stop walking."

He comes bounding over to us, still clapping. He

is just as bouncy and smiley in real life as he is on TV. "Right, guys, tell me what your mission is tonight."

I take a step back so half my face is behind Star Kid.

"We're trying to find a lost dog," Star Kid growls.

"OK," says Casey. "Is that it?"

"Yep," says Star Kid. "You should have been here last week."

Casey seems mildly disappointed for a second, but his enormous, irritating smile soon comes back. "Well, if that's the mission, then that's the mission! Lead on, Amazing Avengers!"

If I felt stupid before, now I feel like King Moron of Moronia, standing around in a costume, whistling for a tiny dog called Tyson in the middle of the night.

Casey gets me to go off in front while he talks to Star Kid one-on-one.

"Don't go too far," Star Kid calls after me. He can tell I'm thinking of running, I know it.

All the focus is on Star Kid, so I try to relax. I can't, though. I hear snatches of the conversation. Mentions of him studying jiu-jitsu. The word "justice" seems to come up a lot.

We walk all the way to the other side of the estate,

by the woods and the concrete trench. Casey comes up to me as we approach.

"So I've just spoken to Star Kid," he says. "He tells me he's proficient in jiu-jitsu, and makes the costumes. So what is it you bring to the team?"

Now there's the million-dollar question. What *do* I bring to the team, exactly? It reminds me of those boy bands Mum is into. You've got the one that does all the singing, the one that's pretty, and then you've got the other one that just sort of bums around in the background. That's me. The replaceable one.

"Moon Boy isn't much of a talker," says Star Kid, coming to my rescue.

"Wow, so you're the spokesperson, too!" says Casey. "You're really carrying the heavy loads here, aren't you, Star Kid?"

Yeah, cheers, Casey. I take the opportunity to walk away a little and escape his shouty clutches. I tread along the edge of the trench. Again, the camera is focused on Star Kid. With a bit of luck, I'll get through this without being on it at all.

Hang on a second. I think I can hear something. I stop and listen, but Casey is still talking.

"Shhh!"

Everyone stops and looks at me. "What is it, Moon Boy?" asks Casey.

"I think I hear something."

It was a thin, whimpering sound. Ah, there it is again.

"You heard that, right?" I ask.

"I think so," says Star Kid. "You think it's Tyson?"

As soon as he says the name, the whimpering gets louder. Now it's a faint yipping noise.

I drop down into the trench. It's slightly louder down here. The more I walk along, the clearer it gets. It sounds kind of echoey. Oh no. I reach the grid over the big drain at the end.

The others come down and Star Kid shines his torch through the bars. The yipping gets louder. I see something skittering around down there.

"So what do we think?" says Casey. "Is that Tyson?"

"Either that or a really angry rat," says Star Kid.

"Hey, Steve, point the camera down there, will you?" says Casey.

The cameraman does as he says. Sure enough, there's Tyson, cowering at the bottom of the shaft.

"Poor little thing must have squeezed through the bars," says Casey.

Star Kid claps. "OK, first things first, we need to

get the grill off. TV boy, you can help, too. Make yourself useful."

Each of us grabs a bar and we begin to pull. It starts to come away in the top left corner, so we all switch positions and yank it free.

"Teamwork! Booyeah!" Casey hoots.

"OK, we need to decide who's going down there," says Star Kid.

We peer over the edge. It's probably a two-metre drop.

"I'll do it," I say, even though I really don't want to. It's time to prove my worth to the team. Besides, it gets me away from the camera.

With the grid removed, there's a slope down to the bottom. Tyson must have slid down it because if he'd fallen from that height, he'd have been badly hurt. I sit down and lie back so I can fit through. I take a few deep breaths. All I have to do is slide down, grab Tyson and climb back out. Don't think about your claustrophobia. Definitely don't think about what else could be lurking down there.

"Be careful, Moon Boy," says Star Kid.

I can do this. Here we go. I take Star Kid's torch, push off from the side and slide down. It stinks down here. Like dank water and sour mud. I find

Tyson standing in a puddle and quickly scoop him up. He snarls and bites my hand like it's made of Pedigree Chum. I'm wearing gloves, but his teeth are as sharp as needles and I can still feel them. I leap on to the slope and drag myself and Tyson up, while he continues to go at my hand. There's gratitude for you. I reach up and post him out into the trench, just to get rid of him, then drag myself out.

"YOU DID IT!" Casey yells. "BOOYEAH, BOOYEAH, BOOYEAH!"

Tyson must have decided he likes the taste of me and runs after me for round two. He leaps at my leg, but I manage to dodge. He tries again. I turn to try and climb out of the trench when—

"AAAAARRGH!" Tyson clamps his teeth on my bum.

I wriggle around trying to get him off, while the camera follows me. Star Kid grabs him and manages to prize him off me.

When Star Kid holds him, he's fine, but still snarls at me. So that's my role in the team. Star Kid is good at fighting and costume design and talking, and I'm good at rescuing tiny dogs that want to kill me.

After we reunite Tyson with his owners, Casey gives us all hugs and bids us goodbye. As he walks away with his crew, he yells, "We're going to air this one as soon as possible because it was so cool. Peace out!"

"I don't know whether that's a good thing or not," I say.

CHAPTER 35

Dad comes home from work in an incredibly cheerful mood. The happiest I've probably ever seen him. He's all, "Good afternoon, family! I've got a surprise for you!"

Millie gasps. "Are we going home?"

His smile downgrades slightly. "No, Millie. As you know, this is our home. At least for the time being. It's still a really cool surprise, though! Get your shoes on and follow me."

We all do as we're told. I look at Mum for a clue, but she's as confused as I am. Dad leads us down the stairs and into the car park.

"Ta da!" he says.

I look around for what he could be talking about. It's literally just a car park.

"Isn't she a beaut?" Dad says.

It's only now I realize what he's talking about. There's a car parked up in the spot right outside the door. I don't know anything about cars, so I don't know what make it is or anything like that, but it's red and it's shiny and it looks nice.

"Pretty!" says Millie. "It looks like a Cherry Zinga!"

"You've bought a car?" says Mum.

"You're a sharp one, aren't you, babe?" Dad laughs. "Well, don't just stand there, everybody get in!"

"Hold on," says Mum. "How could we afford that?"

Dad rolls his eyes. "Why have you always got to kill my buzz? I got it for an incredible price. A steal. And anyway, don't worry about that." He whacks the bonnet. "This little beauty is our ticket to independence. We can get out and about now! Go wherever we want."

"Home?" Millie yelps.

"Except there," says Dad. "Right, what are we waiting for? Everybody in!"

Millie runs and jumps into the back, and I get in next to her. Dad gets in the passenger seat and lets Mum in the driver's side.

"Pretty nice, eh?" he says, grinning.

"I'm not saying it isn't," says Mum. "I'm just worried about how we'll afford it."

Dad groans theatrically. "For the last time, it's all taken care of. Just enjoy the car."

Millie sniffs the air. She's noticed the smell, too.

"Daddy," she says. "It smells like chips in here."

It really does. Chippy chips and batter.

Dad chuckles. "That's probably because I bought it from George at the Fish Bar."

Now he's said that, I remember seeing this car parked around the precinct before. And I get a flashback to when we were in there and George was extra nice to Dad and fried up some fresh cod for him. Maybe that's why? Because Dad was buying his car off him? That must have been it.

"I'll put some air fresheners in, get it valeted; it'll be fresh as the day it was made" says Dad. "Right, what say we take her for a spin?"

"What, now?" asks Mum.

"No, next week. Yes, now!"

"But Millie needs a car seat!"

Dad sighs, all exaggerated like he's acting in a pantomime. "We'll get her one tomorrow. She'll be all right in the normal seat for now."

Mum turns around and looks at us. "What do you think, kids?"

"YAY!" says Millie, already yanking at her seat belt.

Mum fires up the engine. It purrs softly. "Wow," she whispers.

She must know what's going on. If I do, then she must. Even Millie must have an idea. He's done it time and time again. When things are getting a little miserable, he'll go out and buy something big and expensive to put it right. It's how I ended up with my PS5, so I shouldn't moan, but it's so obvious.

As we smoothly glide out of the car park, I realize this is the first time I've been in any vehicle going anywhere since we arrived in the hire van. It feels weird. As we pass the precinct, I see George standing outside the chippy, raising the shutters. Dad sees him too, and he leans over and beeps the horn. George smiles and waves, but when I turn around and watch him as we drive away, I see his shoulders droop and his smile disappear.

"It handles really nicely," says Mum as she pulls it on to the dual carriageway.

"Only the best for this family," says Dad. "Hey, put your foot down a bit; let's see what she can really do."

Mum steps on the gas and we pick up speed, sweeping into the fast lane to overtake a lorry.

"It can really go!" says Mum.

"She can go further," says Dad. "Put your foot down a bit more."

"I'm doing the speed limit," says Mum, pulling back into the left-hand lane.

"So what?" says Dad. "There are no cameras around here. We'll be fine."

"No," says Mum, firmer this time. "The kids are in the back."

Dad tuts and sits back with his arms folded, but in a couple of seconds, he's up again, pointing out of the window.

"Look at that!"

There's a huge lake, stretching off into the distance. Closer to the road, a big sign says: ADVENTURE BOATING LAKE: WATER SKIING, SPEEDBOATS, WINDSURFING.

"How about that?" says Dad. "We'll have to go there one day, hire a boat."

"No thanks," says Mum. "I only have to look at one of those things and I get seasick. Hey, let's go down here." She slows down and turns just past the lake, where a sign says "Abbotsdale welcomes careful drivers."

As we drive further, it's like entering a different world. The houses look like they were built about two hundred years ago. There are ponds and red phone boxes, and in the centre there's a green, as flat and smooth as a pool table. It's even nicer than our old area.

Dad lets out a long whistle. "Look at this place. Very nice."

"It's magical," says Millie, pointing at the church further down. "It looks like a princess lives here."

"One day, perhaps we'll be able to live somewhere like this," says Dad.

Mum laughs. "In our dreams, maybe."

"Keep dreaming," says Dad. "Because I can make it happen. Mark my words."

I think that was supposed to sound reassuring, but it really didn't.

Worry Book

I'm getting serious déjà vu here.

CHAPTER 36

I tip out a tiny bit of my can of Coke and watch it swirl and twirl before splatting against the ground below. Tel and I are sitting on the edge of the underpass, our legs dangling below us. Just ahead, Ronnie's house is being gutted by police. Every few minutes they come out with stuff in clear plastic bags.

"This isn't how I imagined it," says Tel.

"What do you mean?"

"Well, I spent years planning and fantasizing about bringing Ronnie down, and it was always more…" He seems to be searching for the right word. "*Dramatic*."

"It felt dramatic enough to me," I say, fighting off flashbacks of Ronnie's basement.

"You know what I mean, Phineas," says Tel. "I

245

suppose I'd just built him up so much in my mind that when he was removed, I was expecting the entire estate to transform physically. Like, suddenly it would get prettier, like a curse had been lifted. Sometimes I have to remind myself he's just a man."

A couple of people have stopped on the path and are watching, too.

"It doesn't feel real," says Tel. "Like, it might not be over."

"How can it not be over?" I say. "He's gone. And by the sounds of it, he's not getting out any time soon."

"I can't explain it," says Tel, shrugging. "It's just a feeling."

Later on, I'm sitting in the lounge, secretly checking the Avengers site, when Dad bursts in. I can tell he's in one of his good moods.

"Get your glad rags on, family, we're going out!" he yells.

"Why do we have to wear rags?" asks Millie.

Dad laughs and scoops Millie up, making her scream with delight. "I've booked us a table at Fothergill's restaurant. You're going to love it. It overlooks that boating lake. Very fancy."

"Gino told me about that place," says Mum. "He

says it's really expensive."

Dad's cheery expression clouds over for a second before rebounding. "Well, maybe to a poxy café owner it is, but for someone who's just had a huge bonus at work, it's chump change."

"You've had another bonus?" says Mum.

"Yep! A huge one! Remember me telling you about that supervisor? The one I couldn't stand? Well, he's been sacked and guess who they've promoted?"

Mum gasps. "Oh, that's wonderful!"

Dad winks. "Told you. I'm a new man. Right, let's start getting ready. Table's booked at seven."

Mum takes Millie into the bedroom to start doing her hair. She'll probably need me to go in and hold her still in a minute. Dad stands in the middle of the lounge, still grinning. He locks his gaze on me and hits me with a soft jab.

"We're going to be all right, kid," he says. "Just you wait and see."

Dad drives to the restaurant and, as we leave the estate, we pass a police car. Two cops are inside. Dad grins and waves at them. They glare back at him, not returning the wave.

The restaurant was OK.

CHAPTER 37

When I reach the rendezvous point outside the community centre, I find Star Kid pacing nervously. Tonight's job is to investigate who keeps graffitiing Ali's wall. I've got my suspicions. It's been a few nights since we've been out. Tel thought we should keep a low profile for a bit after the Casey Kellman incident, and there hasn't really been much to do anyway.

"Come on, then," I say. "Let's find the phantom tagger."

Star Kid's eyes fall on me, but it's like he's looking through me.

"Everything OK?" I ask.

"We're not doing that tonight," he says. "Something else has come up. Something bigger."

"But there haven't been any messages on the website," I say.

Star Kid reaches into the little bag attached to his belt and pulls out his phone. "A few days ago, I went to the community centre for jiu-jitsu. Pat mentioned this had been put through the door." He hands it over to me. On the screen, there's a crumpled handwritten letter.

Superheroes,
Sorry I had to write this message. I'm embarrassed and a little desperate, but I have no one else to turn to. If I go to the police, I'll be putting myself in danger.

Long story short, someone has taken over from Ronnie. Except he's even worse. He's been doing the rounds of the estate, lending money at sky-high levels of interest. If you miss a payment, he threatens you with bad stuff. Really bad.

I'm sending this note anonymously because I can't risk him finding out it was me. Just do what you can.

Thanks.

"Oh no," I say. "Do you think the police missed one of Ronnie's men?"

Star Kid nods. "I surmised that this man would be doing his rounds in the daytime, so I went out yesterday, in plain clothes, and I saw him. He was going to various addresses around the estate. It had to be him. I followed him at a safe distance all the way."

Star Kid starts walking, so I do too.

"I assumed he didn't live on the estate," he continues. "So I thought I was just going to follow him to a car, and I would take a note of his number plate and continue my investigation from there, but no. He lives here."

"Oh," I say.

We head across the car park.

"So I know where he lives," says Star Kid.

"Is that where we're going now?"

Star Kid nods.

"Right," I say, feeling panic rising in my stomach. "And I can't help but notice we're heading for Ambrose Court."

Star Kid stays silent and opens the door.

"I can't believe it's someone in my block!" I say as we climb past floor one. When we pass two, I say, "I can't believe it's someone on my floor!"

We walk across the landing, and when we stop, as I

deep down knew we would all along, outside my flat, I say, "I can't believe it's someone in my flat!"

Star Kid stares at me, his expression unchanged.

"OK, funny joke," I say. "Where does the real bad guy live?"

"We need to talk," he says.

We're sitting on the roof of Primrose House. I'm struggling not to cry.

"It can't be my dad," I say. "You must have made a mistake. My dad works at a dog food factory. He's a supervisor!"

"You think I like this?" says Star Kid. "You think I wanted it to be your dad? When he opened your front door and went inside, I was devastated."

"But how do you know that's what he's doing?" I say. "He could be going over there for anything."

Star Kid sighs and pulls his phone off his belt. He presses play on a sound file.

"You owe me two hundred today, Marky. Where is it?"

I close my eyes. It's Dad.

"OK, enough."

Dad keeps talking, getting more aggressive.

"ENOUGH," I snap.

Star Kid finally shuts the phone off.

I look down at the cracked concrete far below. It's all making sense now. When he suddenly started coming home happier must have been when he quit the dog food job and started doing what he's doing now. Then there's all those people acting scared of him, and the car. And Ronnie talking about the new bloke he had working for him. He was going to send me out with Dad, wasn't he? How could I not see it? Maybe I didn't want to.

"Now I need you to be honest with me," says Star Kid. "Because if I find out you're lying to me, you are out of the team and I will never speak to you again."

"OK?" I say, my voice wobbling.

"Did you know about this?"

I shake my head. "No. He had been acting weird, but then he always does. I had no idea what was happening."

"Has he ever done anything like this before?" he asks.

Now this one isn't as easy. I could tell him. I could tell him everything. But I can't. That has to remain a secret.

"No," I say, but this time I can't look at him. "No, he's never done this before as far as I know." The burning feeling of guilt in the back of my head is as real as the building I'm sitting on.

"I believe you," says Star Kid. "But we can't let this go on."

"Please," I say. "Don't call the police."

Star Kid seems surprised. If he calls the police, Dad will go to prison, no getting out of it this time, and he'll probably never get out. And what will happen to us?

"Just let me talk to him," I say. "I'll make him see sense."

Star Kid sighs. "All right. We'll try that first. But we can't let this go on much longer."

"It won't," I say. "I promise."

Worry Book

What am I going to do?

What am I going to do?

What am I going to do?

CHAPTER 38

The right time didn't come during breakfast. Mum and Millie were always there, and I didn't have the opportunity. How am I supposed to bring it up, anyway? "Oh, hey, Dad. I hear you've gone back to being a criminal again! Would you mind stopping?"

He puts on his work overalls, picks up his packed lunch and heads out of the door, a spring in his step. Mum smiles.

"I can't remember the last time I've seen him in such a good mood," she says. "That promotion has really helped him."

I say nothing. I know exactly why he's in a good mood and it makes me feel sick. He's had a promotion, but not the kind Mum thinks it is.

When Mum goes to work at Gino's, and Millie

goes to day care, I head out and stalk the estate looking for Dad. It will be easier to confront him if I catch him in the act. Just going up to him out of nowhere at home would be like poking a bear.

I start at the blocks near us and work my way outwards, but I can't find him. Hang on a sec. I head back to our block and the car isn't there. Where is he? Is he parking it somewhere else and coming back, or is he somewhere else altogether? A text from Tel:

Talked to him yet?

Haven't had a chance.

He's typing. He's typing. He's still typing.

You've got til the end of the day.

That's it. What am I supposed to do? I don't know where he is. I start texting Dad, but I can't find the words, so I stop.

I walk around the estate, going over and over in my head what I'll say to Dad and how he'll react, and what I'll say then. I've done this so many times over the years, but somehow, I never manage to predict what he'll do. After another check to see if his car is back, I head home for more rehearsals with the Wall Bears.

Mum brings Millie home from day care. As soon as she gets in, Millie switches on the TV and settles on the sofa with a little bowl of Cherry Zingas. She seems so happy now. A wave of anger at Dad surges through me. How could he be so stupid?

I close my eyes and try and put everything in order. My mind drifts and my arms and legs feel heavy. Dad's face floats by. Then there's Tel, and Ronnie, and Gino, and Mum and Uncle Shane, but then Dad comes back. He's looming over me.

"Why can't you be a man?"

And I'm asking him, "What does that mean? How can I be a man?"

"BOOYEAH!" My eyes snap open. Casey Kellman is in the studio on TV, bouncing around like a kangaroo on energy drinks.

"Hello, you gorgeous people, and welcome to *Amazing Kids*. This week, we're abseiling in Norwich, painting murals in Manchester and skateboarding in Belfast. But first! Did you think superheroes only existed in movies and comic books? Well, you're wrong. In a town called Tammerstone, they are real, and they're doing amazing things! Check it out!"

"Hey, Millie, let's change the channel," I say. Mum is only in the kitchen and might be able to hear it.

"No!" she says, clutching the remote like it's made of gold. "I love this show!"

I see myself on screen as Casey sprints towards us. Even though I'm fully masked, the terror in my face is obvious.

"That's you!" Millie yelps, her eyes huge. "How are you on telly?"

I frantically shush her. "That's our secret, remember? You promised you wouldn't tell anyone."

The front door opens.

"I'm serious, Millie, change the channel," I hiss.

"NO!" she screams.

"What's going on?" says Dad, grinning. "Hang about, isn't that here?"

"Yeah!" says Millie. "I can't believe telly was here!"

Dad plonks himself down on the sofa next to us. "I wonder who they are?"

"I don't know," says Millie, sounding out every word slowly like she's acting in a nativity play. "I have no idea who it is."

Dad laughs a little and shakes his head. "You're a strange one, Mils."

The TV shows us searching for Tyson, then me sitting on the edge of the drain, waiting to go in. And I'm talking. Oh no, I'm talking and it really sounds like me. I thought I was doing a voice, but it's not very strong at all and Dad is looking at me, Dad is looking at me, Dad is looking at me. And Tyson is biting my bum and Millie is laughing, and Dad is looking at me.

The report ends. Dad has stopped looking at me. He's getting up and going into the kitchen. I turn around and see him hugging Mum. Maybe he didn't put two and two together. It's possible. It's very possible. After he breaks off the hug, I see him head towards their bedroom and pull a notebook out of his pocket. It's the same one he came back for that day. I bet he keeps records in there of how much people owe him.

Millie taps my knee. "Did I do good?"

I try and force a smile. "You did great."

"Why didn't you tell me you met Casey?" she says. She looks hurt.

"I'm sorry," I whisper. "We'll talk about it later, OK?"

Dad comes back into the lounge and sits down.

By now, the show has moved on to the abseiling in Norwich.

I leave it a couple of minutes before getting up. I don't want to seem too obvious.

"Off out?" says Dad.

He's smiling, just a little. I don't know what to make of it.

"No," I say. "Just going to my room."

Dad winks at me. "Right you are."

I duck into my room and stand behind the door. I count to ten, then ease the door open and look up and down the landing. Everyone is where they should be. I take two tiptoe steps and enter Mum and Dad's room. Where has he put that book? It's not on the bedside table, or tossed on to the bed. It's got to be in here somewhere. I try the drawer in the bedside table, but there's nothing in there except a book and some cables. I try the other drawers and find only pants and socks. I drop to my knees and look under the bed. Bingo. There it is. Dad's side. If I get this, I'll have proof, something to confront him with.

Footsteps. Fast footsteps. I drop the notebook and make for the door, but it's too late. The door opens.

"What are you doing in here?" says Dad.

"Oh," I say, nudging the book with my foot. "I was just looking for the, um, laptop charger."

"In the lounge," he says.

"Oh," I say. "Oh, right."

I'm trying to leave, but Dad sticks his hand out. "Hold on, son," he says.

Here it is.

"We've not been spending enough time together," he says.

"Haven't we?" I say.

He shakes his head. "I've been thinking we should head over to the boating lake. Make a day of it."

"Maybe," I say.

Dad nods and gently karate chops my arm. "I'll book us in for tomorrow. Bit of father-son time."

I try and think of something, some way to get out of it, but my brain is empty. Tumbleweed.

"OK," I squeak.

Dad grins and ruffles my hair. "Can't wait," he says.

CHAPTER 39

"So, come on, then," says Tel. "What did he say?"

I asked him to meet me by the trench where we found Tyson. It's quiet here. I didn't want to text him to explain and there was no way I could talk on the phone in the flat. Face to face is the only way. I wish it weren't.

The sun is beginning to set, bathing everything in golden light and making it look like the exact opposite of how I feel inside. I take a breath. I did all kinds of rehearsals in my head on the way over here and all of them ended up with Tel freaking out. Here goes nothing.

"I can't do it today," I say.

Tel goes to butt in, but I carry on before he can. "But we're going out tomorrow, just the two of us."

"That's no good, Finn," says Tel. "I said he needed to be stopped today."

I think that was the first time he didn't call me Phineas.

"Oh, what's one more day?" I say, exasperated.

"I know how these people work," says Tel. "He will manipulate you into keeping quiet. Where are you even going, anyway?"

"The boating lake," I reply.

Tel laughs, a single, bitter bark. "So you're going to be alone with him in the middle of a lake? Nowhere to run? Give me a break." He pulls out his phone.

"What are you doing?" I ask.

"I gave you a chance to stop him and you blew it," he says. "Game over."

"No!" I grab his phone and hold it behind my back.

He stares at me, bug-eyed. "What do you think you're doing?"

"I need you to give me more time," I say. "*Please.*"

Tel makes a grab for the phone, but I jump backwards.

"Give it back, Finn." His voice is dark and full of menace.

"I promise you, I will sort it all out tomorrow. I just can't let you call the police."

"Why not?"

How can I tell him? How can I explain that if Dad goes to prison that I don't know what will happen to me, Mum and Millie? We'd probably be moved somewhere else, or just left to get on with things, with no protection.

"Because I'll have no dad, OK?" I say. "Is that what you want?" The words are out of my mouth before I even think them: "You want me to be like you?"

All the air leaves my body and I'm looking at the orange sky. Tel is on top of me, clawing his phone back and holding me down.

"Get off me!" I try to shout.

"My dad did nothing wrong," he growls. "He didn't deserve what happened to him."

"What are you talking about?" I cry.

Something flickers in Tel's eyes and he loosens his grip on me and gets up.

"Just forget it," he says. He starts walking away.

"Tel!" I call after him.

But he doesn't even look back. He's running. I go after him, but he suddenly turns into a network of alleyways, and I've lost him. I call after him again, but he's not coming back.

My head is spinning. I have to find him before it's

too late. I run towards Primrose House, but there's no sign of him.

What did he mean when he said that thing about his dad doing nothing wrong? What happened to his dad?

I find the cemetery gate open, but can't see anyone inside. Maybe I was wrong. I mean, Tel's dad could be alive. It's possible. But I press on.

I don't like cemeteries, especially alone. And it can't be much longer until it goes dark. I'll be as quick as I can. I keep to the middle path and look along each row as I go. It's like looking for Mum in a supermarket, except Mum's not here and everyone's dead.

The graves start off old, with angel statues and headstones worn smooth, but the further back I go, the newer they get. Wait. I can see a figure up ahead, crouched in front of a gravestone. I slow my pace down. I don't want to spook him. By the time I'm behind him, I'm practically tiptoeing.

I see the name on the headstone.

TERRY ALAN CAMPBELL
Beloved father and husband.

"Figured it out then, eh?" says Tel, without turning around. His voice is thick with tears.

"What happened?" I ask.

Tel sniffs and wipes his nose with the back of his hand. "Hit and run," he says. "I was eight years old. Ronnie did it. Everyone knows it. But he got away with it."

I close my eyes. Things are beginning to make sense now. Why he was so desperate to get rid of Ronnie, why he's so obsessed with justice. He's doing it for his dad.

"Why didn't you tell me?" I say.

Tel slowly gets to his feet and turns around. His face is streaked with tears.

I didn't think Tel could cry.

"Poor Tel," he says. "It's all I've heard practically my whole life. I got it from teachers, I got it from social workers, I got it from kids at school, the nicer ones anyway, and when someone new showed up, it felt like I could have a new start: a new identity. Someone who wouldn't say *poor Tel*. I've had enough of pity. Pity gets you nowhere. I want real change. So something like this can't happen again."

"I promise you," I say. "I will talk to my dad tomorrow and I will get him to stop. You have my word."

Tel runs a hand down his face and looks up at the darkening sky. When he finally locks eyes with me, he nods. "OK," he says. "Tomorrow."

Worry Book

What if Dad says no?

What if I'm not brave enough?

CHAPTER 40

"Look at this bad boy," says Dad as we approach the boat. "Speed King Three. Pretty cool, eh?"

I'm no expert on boats, but even so, it looks like a good one. It's dark blue with a white stripe along the side. There's probably room for about four people on there, but it's just me and dad. Father-son bonding, just like he said.

I have a big orange life vest on, which comes up to my ears. Not the ideal outfit for having the big talk with Dad. Then again, what would be the ideal outfit? A suit of armour?

The lake seems far bigger than I remember, even from when we had dinner in the restaurant. It stretches far off into the distance. I've never done anything like this before. Dad took me fishing once years ago, but he got bored after a while and took me home. Then went out on his own. He didn't say where.

We climb inside and Dad fires up the engine. "Whoa, what a beast!" he yells over the roar. "Let's see what she can do!"

I sit down and hold tight as Dad tears out of the dock at top speed, sending spray flying in all directions. Dad whoops and cheers as he steers wildly. I grip the seat so hard my hands hurt.

"Maybe slow down a bit!" I yell.

"What?" says Dad.

"I SAID MAYBE SLOW DOWN, I'M GOING TO FALL OUT!"

Dad slows down, laughing. "All right, all right. You know me, Damian, I'm a speed freak."

"It's Finn," I say.

Dad laughs. "Mate, we're in the middle of a lake. There's no one here." He turns around and sticks his arms out. "DAMIAN! MY SON'S NAME IS DAMIAN!"

I want to disappear into my life vest like a tortoise into its shell.

"Anyway, you want a go?" he says, pointing at the steering wheel.

I shake my head. "The bloke in the hut said only over eighteens can operate these things."

Dad looks at me like I've beamed down from Planet Bedwetter. "Well, what the bloke in the hut don't know won't hurt him. Come on, I'll stand next to you."

"No," I say. "I'll just be the passenger."

"Come on," he says again, and this time his tone makes it clear it's not a request.

I grip the side and push myself up. What do cartoon pirates call people who are no good on boats? Landlubbers? Well, I am a landlubber. Big time. There is no one who lubs land more than me.

"It's easy," says Dad. "All you do is push this lever like this." The boat starts moving across the lake. "Hold the steering wheel."

I do as he says.

"How about that?" he yells. "Great, isn't it?"

It kind of is. I'm in control of this big, powerful thing blasting over the water. As we pick up speed, we bounce on the ripples and my stomach jumps, too. Dad grabs the wheel and steers us towards some windsurfers, sending huge waves skidding over them. I can't help but laugh. I shouldn't, but it's so funny. For a few seconds, I forget about everything.

Dad is just Dad; I am just me. There are no secret identities.

We stop for lunch at the far end of the lake. Mum made us sandwiches: beef for Dad, cheese for me. She knows exactly how I like them. The sun is properly out now, but the gentle breeze coming off the water means it's not too sweaty.

"This is the life, eh?" says Dad. "You know, when we first moved here, I was fed up. I felt penned in by all that concrete. But now we've got the car, we can get out to places like this. Hopefully, we'll be able to get out into the country before long, live somewhere really nice."

This is the time, this is the time. I need to get my mouth ready to form the words. Go, go, g—

"I know you're one of those superheroes, son," says Dad.

What? Did he really just say that?

"N-no," I say. "I don't know what you're talking about."

Dad sits forward, elbows on knees, hands clasped. He doesn't have his life vest on. He took it off ages ago. My legs are shaking and the heels of my shoes are tapping on the bottom of the boat.

"I found the costume, Damian."

I close my eyes. This can't be happening.

"And even if I hadn't found it, a blind man on a galloping horse could see that was you on that TV show," he says.

Is this why he wanted to get me on a boat? To get me away from everyone and everything so he could have it out with me?

"We're supposed to be in hiding, Damian," he says. "New identities. And you're prancing around on telly. What are you trying to do to us?"

"I'm wearing a mask," I say. "No one would be able to tell it was me. Plus, I don't think Uncle Shane watches kids' TV."

"Sure," says Dad. "But if you carry on, you're going to get more and more famous, and they are going to find out who you are. It's only a matter of time. And when they find out, Shane will find out. And that's bad news for all of us."

"You know what else is bad news?" I say.

This is it. This is it. I'm doing it.

"What?" says Dad.

"Yougoingaroundlendingmoneywhenyou'resupposed tobeatwork." I say it so fast it comes out as one word. I stare at the floor of the boat, watching a trickle of water

271

pushing and pulling a speck of mud with the rocking of the waves.

"What are you talking about?" asks Dad.

"Someone reported you to us," I say. "We know."

We sit in silence for a few seconds, facing each other as the rippling lake gently rocks the boat.

"They must have made a mistake," he says, trying to laugh. "It was probably some bloke that looks like me."

"We have a recording, Dad," I say, still unable to look at him.

Dad goes quiet again, then I feel his hand grip my knee. It's tight. Uncomfortable.

"Who reported me?" Dad's voice is dark and it makes me feel sick.

"It was anonymous," I say. "How long has it been going on?"

Dad takes his hand off my knee. When I finally dare to look at him, his head is in his hands. He scrubs at his hair then snaps back upright. "Few weeks. A month. I don't know."

"If you get caught, you'll go to prison," I say.

Dad sighs. "I'm not cut out for civilian work. I can't stand there packing dog food and getting paid peanuts. I wasn't made for that. I'm ... I'm better than that. I need to make enough money to get us out of here."

A couple of old blokes row past us on a little wooden boat. One of them calls hello, but Dad ignores him.

"Were you working for Ronnie?" I ask.

Dad smiles, and I hate it. It's this smug grin. I've seen it a million times, mostly when he's arguing with Mum and he thinks he's got the better of her.

"Yeah, I was, but the plan was always to take over. He was a chump. When you got him sent down, I was happy as Larry. Of course, I didn't know it was you back then. See, the problem with Ronnie is that he was too small time, too sentimental. He had enough money to move off the estate and get people's eyes off him, but he didn't. He stayed. I won't make that mistake. I'm cleverer than that. I mean, having meetings in his own house? That's asking to be caught."

He sits there, looking impressed with himself. Now I really want to throw up.

"It's how we ended up with the car, isn't it?" I ask. "You took it from George."

Dad's smile disappears and his glare snaps on to me. "I did not *take* it. Not like that. George is an adult who borrowed money from me. He put the car up as collateral. When he couldn't pay me back, the car became mine. We made a deal. Maybe when you grow up and stop playing superheroes, you'll understand."

I allow myself a second to focus. I can't let him intimidate me. I have to stay strong. "Look, Dad," I say, "you know there's proof of what you're doing. You're going to get caught."

"You underestimate me," says Dad. "I haven't got that many clients on my books. It won't take much work to figure out which one of them is the snitch. Then it will just be a case of having a word with them and straightening things out."

I swallow hard. "It's not that easy. The recording has been passed on to someone else. Not a client. And they have backups."

I see his jaw clench. I've seen that look so many times. It's never good. "Then you've got to tell me who this is and where they're keeping them."

"I can't," I say. "I don't even know who it is. They won't tell me."

Of course, I know it's Tel, but I'm not going to admit it. I focus on the water rippling behind Dad. The flat, calm water.

"You can't talk to them?"

I shake my head. "Like I said, they're anonymous. But they did say that they won't release the evidence on one condition: if you stop doing what you're doing. All of it."

Dad looks around like he's scoping out an escape. "OK," he says. "OK, OK. How about this?" He clasps his hands together with his index fingers sticking out, like a gun. "I'll stop doing what I'm doing. There will be no more business in our area. So if they get in touch again, you can tell them that. But you need to stop going out being a superhero. It's too risky."

I've loved being Moon Boy. It's given me something to get out of bed for in the morning. But if it's going to put us in danger, it has to stop.

"OK," I say. "If that's what it will take."

Dad nods and sticks out his hand. "We're going to be all right, son."

I take it. I hope he's right.

CHAPTER 41

I'm standing on the bridge over the dual carriageway, watching the cars zoom underneath me. I remember Colt's game and try to guess where they're going, but my imagination isn't firing up today, and I can't think of anything.

I hardly slept last night. I just lay there, one hand tucked under the pillow, staring at the ceiling and wondering what I'm going to do now. It didn't pay off because I'm still no closer to knowing. I guess when I start school in September, I'll be busier with homework and things like that, which will pass the time. It's a depressing thought.

I hear footsteps coming up the steps, so I straighten up. It's Tel.

I feel nearly as nervous as when I had it out with Dad, and the feeling only gets worse the closer Tel gets.

"So?" he says.

I want to tell him face to face, so he can see Dad isn't telling me what to say. I want him to know I'm telling the truth.

I try and read Tel's body language: all closed off and confrontational. I think he's expecting me to tell him I can't stop Dad. Let's see how he takes it.

"Dad is going to stop doing what he's doing," I say.

Tel's expression brightens slightly. "Seriously?"

I nod. "I told him there was proof that could be sent to the police and he promised he'd stop. But there's something else."

"What?" says Tel.

I take a breath. "I've also agreed that I won't do the superhero thing any more."

"What?!" he says again.

"It's complicated," I say. "But there are reasons."

"Such as?"

I run a hand down my face. I've rehearsed my lines for this like it's a school play, but now I'm actually here, in front of the audience, the stage lights making me sweat, it's not that easy.

"Dad says it's too dangerous for me to be out there late at night," I say. "And to be fair, he's got a point. I mean, you're a trained fighter. You can defend yourself. What can I do if I get in trouble?"

"I don't get it," says Tel. "How did he even find out?"

"Casey Kellman," I say. "Dad saw that show and knew it was me, straight away. And then…" I take a moment to pull myself together. "And then he went snooping in my room and found the costume."

Tel closes his eyes and bows his head.

"Look," I say. "We can still be friends. We can still hang out. I … I love hanging out with you. I just can't be part of the team any more, that's all. I mean, it's not as if I ever did anything useful, is it? You'll be fine without me."

Tel opens his eyes and looks me right in the face. He doesn't do that often. "It was never about your technical ability, Phineas. That kind of thing can be taught, in time. It was about your heart." He gingerly reaches out and rests his hand in the middle of my chest. My shoulders start to tremble and I don't know why. "You can learn to fight, but you can't learn having a good heart."

Great, now I'm going to cry again.

We hug and agree to see each other again over the summer. I'm happy I'm not losing him as a friend, but I know deep down that things will never be the same between us. But, if it keeps Dad from going back to his old ways, it will be worth it.

Worry Book

I'm really going to miss being an Ampleforth Avenger.

CHAPTER 42

The days go by slowly when there's nothing to look forward to. Mum goes to Gino's, Millie goes to day care, Dad goes to work. He told me he's got his job at the dog food factory back.

"It was a blip, son," he says. "I'm back on the straight and narrow now."

It's been a week since I stopped being Moon Boy. I've been messaging Tel and asking him how he's getting on, but it's not the same. He's been going out every night. Sometimes, I'll look out of the window and try to spot him, but I haven't managed it so far.

So now I'm lying in bed. It's earlier than normal, but I've got nothing else to do. Millie is having one of those nights when she just won't go to sleep.

"What's two plus two plus two plus three plus one million thousand?"

"Can you run faster than a tiger?"

Then she'll quieten down and her breathing will go slow, when all of a sudden:

"If a robot cries, does oil come out?"

"I don't know, Mils," I say. "Probably. Then again, if a robot has human feelings, what its tears are made of should be the least of your worries."

Millie sighs, then turns over and stares at me, her eyes shiny in the half-dark. "I'm sad," she says.

I prop myself up on my elbow. "Why are you sad?"

"Because I wrote Santa a letter and it didn't come true," she says, squeezing the jolly old Saint Nick toy in her arms.

Oh man.

"Well, it was kind of big for Santa," I say. "But maybe he has made it come true in a different way,"

"What do you mean?" she asks.

"Well, maybe you feel like *here* is home now," I say.

Millie's bottom lip sticks out. "But my old bedroom and the garden aren't here."

"True," I say, "but your family is. And all the new friends you've made at day care."

"So you think Santa did that for me?"

"Sure," I say. "After all, he's magic, right?"

Millie gives the toy a kiss on his rosy cheek. "Yeah."

"All right," I say. "Time to go to sleep."

Millie closes her eyes, and soon her breathing is slow again, and her mouth has dropped open slightly. Is it really happening? Is she finally drifting off?

BZZZZZZZZ. BZZZZZZZZ.

My phone vibrates on the bedside table. I snatch it up before it wakes Millie. Tel is calling me. What could he want?

"Hello?"

"I know you've retired, but I need you," he says.

"Why? What's happening?"

"It's kind of embarrassing."

I sit up. "What is it?"

"Well, I responded to a tip-off that someone was using the public toilets for nefarious purposes," he says. "And, well, it seems I've been hoodwinked."

"Hoodwinked?"

"Look, I've been locked in, all right?" he says. "And it really stinks in here."

"Who did it?"

Tel hesitates, like he's ashamed of telling me. "Jay and Dylan."

Ugh. Those idiots. "Can't you just call the police?"
I say.

"I'll be here all night waiting for them," he says.
"I need you."

I sigh, and look over at Millie. She's sound asleep
now.

"OK, fine."

"But suit up," says Tel. "If you come in your
civvies, you could compromise my secret identity."

"One last time," I say.

"One last time."

I know this is breaking my promise to Dad, but it's
an emergency, and it really is going to be my last time.

I carefully drag the costume I thought I'd never
wear again from under the bed and put it on. I stop
and listen. It sounds like Mum and Dad are asleep,
too. Good. I'm sure I won't be long. I'm about to
climb out of the window, but then I remember Jay
and Dylan could be lurking by the public toilet,
waiting for me, so I creep into the lounge and pick
up Dad's baseball bat. They won't mess with me if
I've got that.

The public toilets are at the far end of the precinct.
I have no idea how Dylan and Jay would have got hold
of a key for the place. Probably stole it.

I hammer the door and Tel hammers back. "Is that you, Moon Boy?"

"Yep," I say. "Now, how am I supposed to get in here?"

"Try and kick the door in," says Tel. "I'll stand back."

Now, I've seen this done loads of times in the movies. I've been on the other side of the door when it's happened in real life, too. It doesn't look that hard. I draw up my right foot, surely the stronger of the two, and give the door a kick right by the lock. It shudders, but doesn't give way. I try again, this time harder, but nothing happens.

Laughter echoes across the precinct. I turn around and can already tell it's Jay and Dylan walking towards me.

"I knew he'd come and try and save his mate," says Jay.

"What have you done to Colt, you weirdo?" says Dylan as they draw closer.

I hold the bat in front of me. "What?"

"Ever since you busted him for nicking from the shop, he hasn't wanted to come out with us," says Jay. "You changed him."

"Good," I say. "It proves he's not as stupid as you. Now give me the key."

Jay laughs. "Nah. You're the wussiest one, even with the bat."

My brain whirls and I'm zooming back, like I've jumped in the DeLorean with Doc Brown, back to about three years ago.

I'm bowling with Dad and Uncle Shane. Then as now, I have no idea why Uncle Shane is there, but he's there and it's fun because Uncle Shane always is. At the end of the game, it's Uncle Shane first, me second and Dad third. Dad is in a stinking mood about it. He's blaming the ball, the lane, everything. Uncle Shane isn't having it and is rinsing him mercilessly about his eleven-year-old son beating him at bowling.

Dad is silent all the way home, and when we're home, he goes straight to my bedroom and throws all my action figures out on to the landing. Millie, who is only a baby, starts wailing and Mum asks what he's doing.

He says, "The boy needs to grow up. He's too soft."

And I'm like, "What do you mean? Is this because I beat you at bowling?"

But he doesn't talk to me, he directs it all at Mum. "All this fantasy stuff is pathetic. He's supposed to be carrying on the Butcher name and he's nothing but a crybaby."

He's talking about when this older kid was giving me a hard time at school and instead of, as he put it, "sorting them out", I told a teacher. He always talks about that.

And now, proving his point entirely, I'm standing next to my pile of toys, crying. And Dad's saying something like, "And this is my son", just like he did when he ripped up Tel's comics. And Mum's telling him to stop being horrible, but he's not listening and—

SNAP. Back to the present. I grip the bat extra hard and run at them, watching in real time as their expressions change from smug to concerned to terrified. They back off, but I keep coming and I know this sounds bad, but I am grinning behind this mask. I feel alive, I feel like someone again. How's about this for fantasy stuff, Dad?

"All right, fine!" exclaims Dylan. He drops the key on the floor. "Take it! Take it!"

I slow down to a stop and stand watching them running away, still grinning, knowing how creepy it must look but not caring. It did the job. I scoop up the key and open the door. Star Kid bursts out in a fetid stink cloud. He claps me on the back, then shudders.

"Thanks, Moon Boy," he says. "To be honest. I'm embarrassed that I was so easily fooled."

I shrug. "It's fine. Hopefully they won't bother you again." When I turn to go home, he calls after me.

"This is why I need you," he says.

I stop and close my eyes before turning around. "You know I can't."

He nods. "Yes, I know. But maybe just stay out a bit later tonight?"

I'm still shaking from the thrill of chasing off Jay and Dylan. Even if I went home, there's no way I'd be able to sleep now.

"OK," I say. "But just for tonight."

CHAPTER 43

It's just after midnight when I finally head back to the flat. Nothing much happened after I freed Star Kid from the toilet. We just walked around and talked. It was fun. I'm going to miss it. Of course, I could always sneak out again like I did tonight, but I made a deal with Dad and tonight was an emergency.

When I get back, the window isn't locked. I was in a hurry when I left, after all. I climb back inside, quickly take off my costume and shove it under the bed. While I pull on my pyjama bottoms, I check on Millie. She's not there. What? Maybe she's just gone to the toilet? I tiptoe along the landing, but the toilet door is open and it's empty.

OK, don't panic. Maybe she had a nightmare and

got in with Mum and Dad. She's done that before, back at home. As quietly as I can, I stick my head around their bedroom door. It's too dark to see if she's in there or not. She must be, though. Where else could she be?

I go back to my room and sit on the bed. Millie has to be in there. She has to be. I lie down and close my eyes.

No. No, I can't sleep. I need to know that she's in there. I'm going to have to make sure.

I go to Mum and Dad's room again and look, hoping that my eyes will get used to the dark and I'll see her outline under the bed sheets, between Mum and Dad. But there's nothing. I see nothing.

"What's up?"

Dad's voice makes me jump. I didn't know he was awake.

"Is Millie in here?"

A lamp comes on. I can see the bed. There's Mum, there's Dad. No Millie. No Millie.

"What's going on?" says Mum, squinting.

"Millie's gone," I say.

Mum shoots out of bed and runs into our room.

Dad gets out of bed slowly and walks over to me. He doesn't seem that worried. He stands opposite me and squeezes my shoulders with both hands. "Where were you?" he asks.

I don't know what to say. Mum screaming in the other room gives me a chance to get away.

"She's gone! She's gone!"

"Look, don't panic," says Dad. "She probably just climbed out of the window. She can't have gone far. Let's get out and look for her."

We head straight out into the night to search for her. She was talking about wanting to go home. Maybe she was half asleep and climbed out to try and find home? Maybe all the upset has made her start sleepwalking? I mean, she wandered off before, who's to say that hasn't happened again?

Mum is frantic, calling her name across the dark car park. "Millie? Millie baby, come out now, this isn't funny, darling."

A ground floor door opens behind me and Gino comes out in his dressing gown, along with Lola.

"What's going on?" he says to me.

"Millie's gone missing," I say.

"Again?" Gino asks, eyebrows raised.

"She's just wandered off," says Dad. "She'll turn up. No need for you to get involved."

Gino runs back into his flat and comes out with

a torch. He sees Mum and gives her a quick hug. "Try not to worry, love, I'm sure she's around here somewhere. When did she go missing?"

Dad turns on me. "Good question. When did she go missing, Finn?"

I can't look at him. I think I'm going to throw up. "Sometime between ten thirty and twelve."

Gino gets his phone out of his dressing gown pocket. "I'll call the police, you lot carry on searching, and try not to panic, OK?"

I can't think straight. I check the park, but she's not there.

I check the precinct. It's empty.

I check the park again because I forgot I've already been there. This is my fault. This is all my fault.

I go to the garages where she ended up the first time she walked off, but there's no one there.

A police car arrives, and Mum's having a panic attack, and Dad's angry, and they search the estate, and they don't find her and they don't find her and they don't find her.

CHAPTER 44

I had to give a statement to a police officer. His name was PC Foxton. He was short and round and bald and I don't think he liked me very much.

"So, you snuck out of the flat and left the window open?" he said.

And what else could I say? That's exactly what happened. The CCTV right outside our block wasn't working, and there's no trace of her anywhere. Someone on the first floor said they saw a little girl walking across the car park with someone, but she couldn't see clearly because it was dark. That's all they have. How are they supposed to find her with that?

A doctor had to come out and sedate Mum. That was when Dad found me. He pointed into my room, which was only just open after being dusted for prints and who knows what else.

"We had a deal, Damian," he said, his voice even and low. "I lived up to my end. If you'd done the same, none of this would have happened."

I want to cry, but I can't because that's all I've done for about fifteen hours and I've got no tears left.

"It was an emergency," I croaked.

"More important than your little sister?" he said.

I've got nothing to say. I just want to wake up from this nightmare.

"The police think it might be something to do with Shane," said Dad. "They're investigating that angle. And if it is him, I reckon I know how he found out where we're living."

I sat on the bed and covered my ears. I couldn't listen to any more. He carried on, so I pressed my hands down harder until his voice was a distant rumble. He tried to prize them away, but gave up and left me, slamming the door behind him.

We have a police officer assigned to the flat. She's been here since Millie went missing, which I think is a day. Or two days. Without sleep, I'm losing track. She's a bit nicer than PC Foxton. Her name is PC Spence, but she insists we call her Sharon.

She makes cups of tea and does things around the flat for Mum.

Journalists started to arrive on the estate earlier. With the window open, I can hear them doing their reports in the car park.

"Police say they're hopeful of finding the little girl, but the more time that passes, the less likely her safe return becomes."

While this all happens, Mum just sits in the chair, staring at the Wall Bears, hovering somewhere between asleep and awake.

My phone buzzes. It's been going all day, but I couldn't bring myself to answer it. Now, though, Dad is down the police station and Mum is asleep, so I pick up.

"Finn, oh my life, are you OK?" asks Tel.

"No," I say. "Funnily enough, I'm not OK."

"I'm so sorry this has happened."

"You should be," I say. "If it weren't for you, it wouldn't have."

There's a voice inside my brain, a tiny, nagging voice, which tells me I'm only passing blame on to him because I can't take the full weight of it myself, but I ignore it.

"I want to help you put it right," he says.

"And how can you do that?" I ask.

"I'm going to help you find her."

"Oh, and you can do that, can you?"

"*We* can do it," says Tel. "Both of us."

"What am I supposed to do?"

"People need to see us out there. It's important for morale."

"Seriously?" I drop my voice to a whisper. "You want me to go out there playing superheroes when my sister is missing, probably taken by ... by who knows what kind of sicko? No way!"

"This is not 'playing superheroes', Finn," he says. "When something like this happens, it turns everyone's lives upside down. We need to be out there showing that we're consistent, and that good people do exist. I ... I needed something like that when Dad died."

I screw my eyes shut and rub at my forehead. I need to give Tel a break. He didn't know this would happen. But I can't be Moon Boy. Not after what happened.

"You go out, then. Be Star Kid. But I'm done. It's not worth it any more."

Worry Book

Everything. Just everything.

CHAPTER 45

I managed to get out last night, as me, not Moon Boy. Despite what Tel said, no one bothered me. I kept my hood up and my head down. I just wanted to help the search.

Dad was still at the police station and Mum was being looked after by Sharon, so I quietly left through the front door and walked past the two police officers on constant watch in the car park without being stopped.

I walked the estate, looking for any kind of clue, but found nothing. There were others out, too. Pat had organized volunteers into search shifts, so there are always at least a few people looking. I saw Gino with Lola on a lead, walking through the woods. I think it's the first time I've ever seen him without a smile on his face.

I kept looking around corners, expecting to see Uncle Shane lurking there, like some kind of vampire, but try as I might, I can't imagine him doing something like this. I know he did some bad stuff but surely nothing this bad.

Sharon has gone home for a rest now, leaving us alone for the first time. There are still police outside, though. They're going nowhere. I don't know if that's standard or if it's because of who we are.

I'm sitting in the lounge with Mum. She isn't talking, just staring straight ahead, shaking. Dad has made breakfast, but the toast is burned and I'm not hungry anyway.

"I was talking to a copper last night," says Dad, standing over us with a tea towel slung over his shoulder. "And he says we should start one of those funding pages, you know, get donations to help the search."

Mum doesn't respond. I don't think she even knows he's there.

"Anyway, I've set one up," he says. "I've got some lads from work to spread the word on the internet and what have you. I've already given an interview to the news as well."

"Hold on," I say. "Are you supposed to be going on TV like that?"

"They blurred my face out," he says. "And anyway, it doesn't matter. I'd do anything to get her back."

Suddenly, Mum makes this noise. It's a noise I've never heard her make before. A noise I've never heard anyone make before. It's like a cry and groan mixed together. I put my arm around her, but it's no good. The noise gets louder and she sounds like a wounded animal. I don't know what to do to stop it. I look to Dad for help, but he just disappears into the kitchen and comes back with a glass of water and a couple of pills.

"They must be wearing off," he says to me, placing them into her mouth one by one and getting her to choke them down with the water.

Is this what life is going to be for her? Being dosed up to stop her feeling pain? How long is that supposed to last?

When Mum falls asleep, I go to the laptop and quickly find this fundraiser Dad has set up. It's already raised five thousand pounds. I scroll through the messages left by donors.

Praying for you, little angel.
It's not much but I hope it helps. Xx

Stuff like that. I can't help but cry when I read them. How can some people be so good and others so bad? It makes no sense.

I see a lot of people talking about praying. I've never really done that. Well, besides at weddings and things like that. I mean, it might be worth a go. With Dad back in the kitchen, scrolling through his phone, I close my eyes and start praying. I keep the words in my head because I guess if God is real, he can read your thoughts. Hold on, is that just when you're praying? I wouldn't want him reading my thoughts at any other time. That's private stuff. Anyway, let's go.

Hi God, it's Finn. Or Damian. I don't know which one you'd know me as. I was christened under the name Damian, so maybe that's the one you know. Anyway, I'm sorry I haven't been in touch before. No disrespect to you, I just forget. You probably know about my sister, Millie. People have been praying to you a lot about her. She's missing and it's my fault. I just want her to come home, God. I want her to be safe. I want her to be alive. Because if she's not, I don't know what I'm going to do. I know she has Santa with her, and that's something. I hope that's helping her. Look, I don't know if this is how it works and I don't want

you to get offended if I'm treating you like some kind
of glorified messenger, but can you pass something on
to her for me?

Hi Mils. I just want to say I'm sorry. I'm your big
brother and I was supposed to protect you and I didn't.
I wasn't there when you needed me the most and I
will never forget that for the rest of my life. I … I just
need you to know that we all love you, and we all miss
you, and we are doing our best to find you. So keep
hugging Santa and before you know it, you'll be back
home with us.

OK, God, that's it. Thanks for listening. I know you
must get loads of these and you can't deal with all of
them, but if you could move this one to the top of your
pile, I'd really appreciate it. What is it I'm supposed
to say now? Ah, that's it.

Amen

There's a knock at the door. I look out of the window
and see Gino and a police officer. I go around and
open it. Gino is carrying a big, covered tray.

"Hey, Finn, how are you holding up?" he asks.

I don't know how to answer that. How *am* I
holding up?

"You know," I say with a shrug.

Gino nods like he understands. "I've brought you some sandwiches from the café. I know you probably don't feel like eating, but you need to keep your strength up."

I take the tray, but, before I can say anything, Dad stomps through the lounge and stands behind me.

"Here's Neighbourhood Watch," he says. "Come for a gawp, have you?"

If Gino is bothered, he's doing a good job of hiding it. "I just wanted to see how you all were."

"How do you think we are?" says Dad. "Our little girl is missing. Anyway, I can't see Natasha being back at work. You might want to advertise for a new member of staff."

"I'll keep her job open," says Gino. "I'm not going to make her unemployed on top of everything else."

"Well, aren't you a sweetheart?" says Dad, sarcastically. "Thanks for the sandwiches."

And with that, he shuts the door. I want to ask him why he's so rude to Gino, but the way he's acting, talking to him would be a bad idea. I put the tray down on the kitchen counter and check on Mum. She's asleep again now. Until the next time the pills wear off, at least.

CHAPTER 46

I had a text from Tel earlier.

> Had a thought. Is there anyone you can think
> of who might want to harm the family in some
> way?

What am I supposed to say to that? "Well, actually, my dad used to be part of a criminal gang and in order to escape a prison sentence, agreed to give evidence against them and now we've had to move to a different town and take on new identities, so it's possible someone, maybe a guy called Uncle Shane, who isn't even my real uncle, who has been on the run from the law for the best part of a year, has tracked us down and taken Millie as revenge"?

No. Can't think of anyone.

What about the people who owed him
money? I know about Mark, who we recorded,
but I've not seen anything suspicious around
his flat.

Now, there's a thought. There's no way he'd have told
police about people who owe him because he'd have
to reveal his illegal dealings. Wouldn't it be possible
that someone who couldn't pay might get desperate
and try to get back at him?

I only know one person who owed him:
George.

George from the chippy?

Yeah. He couldn't pay Dad back, so now we
have his car.

I see that Tel is typing, then stopping, typing, then
stopping. I can see his face right now, horrified,
furious. He's probably typing out an angry reply
then changing his mind about it, rewording it again

and again. After a few minutes, his reply finally arrives.

Well, I don't think George would do something like that, but you never know, I suppose. We should head over and talk to him.

Another text arrives straight afterwards.

And when I say "we", you know what I mean.

I didn't want to suit up again, but I want to talk to George and I can't do it as me. I snuck past the police, changed into my costume in the toilets and met Tel at Primrose House.

It's getting late now and we're heading over to the chippy. I don't feel right about this, but I have to at least try something. We find George closing up. When he sees us approaching, he does a double take.

"Crikey, I thought I was being robbed, then," he says.

"We're looking for the girl," says Star Kid.

"You and everyone else in the country," says George.

"We understand you owed Mr Jacobs money and he took your car," says Star Kid.

George's eyes dart between the two of us. "How do you know about that?"

We don't answer.

"Hey, I didn't have anything to do with it," he says. "I mean, I'm not keen on the bloke, but I'd never hurt one of his kids. Besides, when she went missing, I was in here with Debbie. If there's anyone you want to look at, it's old Mary."

Star Kid cocks his head to one side. "Bloody Mary?"

"Yeah, the hoarder," says George. "I saw Chris having a screaming row with her the other night."

My blood turns to ice as I remember what Colt said about her. *She eats kids.*

"What was it about?" I ask.

"I don't know. I only caught the end of it," says George. "But she was ranting something like, 'I put a curse on you and your family.' Gave me the creeps."

"We'll look into it," says Star Kid. "Thank you, George."

We head over to Ivatt Road. Could Bloody Mary

have taken Millie? Could I rule out her following Dad home, waiting in the night and snatching Millie through the open window?

The house is in darkness when we arrive outside, and the piles of stuff are black shadows in the windows. I imagine Millie in there. She'd be so scared.

"Let's go and take a look," says Star Kid, pulling his torch out of his belt.

We carefully walk up the garden path, dodging the overhanging branches and weeds. Star Kid signals that we should go around the back, so I follow him along a path which runs down the side of the house. There is a rusty old bike and a lawnmower and something covered in plastic sheeting, which we have to step around.

The back garden is even worse than the front, with grass taller than us.

"It's like a jungle," Star Kid whispers, shining his torch around. At the end of the garden, there's a shed that has been completely swamped by greenery, the wooden sides buckled and distorted by the thick branches. It's like seeing what the world would look like with no humans, nature starting to reclaim everything.

"Hey," Star Kid whispers. "Look at this!"

I go over to a wooden door with glass panels in the top at the back of the house. One of the panels is missing. Star Kid shines his torch through the hole, into the darkness. Inside there's what appears to be a utility room; there's a washing machine like something from a museum underneath a counter piled high with boxes, books, takeaway leaflets and old crockery.

There is one clear space on the counter, like a small gap between skyscrapers, but when I peer closer, I see there actually is something there: newspaper clippings. There must be about six of them. I squint to try and make out what the top one says.

Girl, aged four, goes missing from estate

Why would she be saving newspaper clippings about Millie's disappearance? The one underneath is sticking out slightly and it looks like it's about her, too. A chill fills my body from top to bottom. What if she really is here?

"OK," Star Kid whispers. "We need to strategize."

But I haven't got time. I reach through the missing panel and open the door from the inside.

"Moon Boy, what are you doing?" Star Kid hisses.

"If this crazy old woman has my sister, I'm going to get her," I say. "Now, you can either come with me or you can go home."

As I step inside, I hear him right behind me. The house has a smell. I know every house has one, but this is beyond that. It's deep, so thick you can almost see it hanging in the air. There's a surprising sweetness to it that seems to whoosh up your nose and stickily cling to the sides. I tell myself that she does not eat kids and that the idea is ridiculous, but I can't eject it from my head.

A mouse darts across the floor in front of me and hides behind a pile of decaying boxes. The utility room leads to a small hallway with some stairs on the left-hand side. There's a small cupboard under there and I don't know why, but I find myself drawn to it. If you were going to hide a little girl, what better place to do it?

I grab the handle and open the door, but Millie isn't in there. But wait.

"Oh," I hear Star Kid say.

Inside the cupboard is the cleanest part of the house we've seen so far. Star Kid's torch illuminates the contents one by one: a tiny table with a pink toy tea set on it. A small, flower-painted chair. And behind, in the corner, an old doll's house. There is no chill running through my body now, just a pure, white-hot rage.

"MILLIE!" I yell. "IT'S ME, DAMIAN! I'M HERE FOR YOU!"

I stomp through the house, flipping on switches that cast a pale, sickly light across the cluttered rooms. I march into what looks like the living room, although I don't see how anyone could live here.

"MILLIE!"

Star Kid runs after me, trying to quieten me down and I watch his face turn from concern to horror.

A high, thin squeal cuts through the air, and then my leg hurts. It really hurts.

CHAPTER 47

I clutch my throbbing calf and hobble over to Star Kid. Mary stands there, pointing a cane at us. It's long and gnarled and dusty. Mary's white hair sticks out from her head, and her mouth, completely toothless, is set in a mean grimace.

"What are you doing in my house?" she demands.

"You have my—" I stop and correct myself before I go too far. "That little girl, don't you? Where is she?"

"What are you talking about?" she asks, still brandishing the cane.

"We saw the newspaper clippings!" I say. "And the little tea set and doll's house under the stairs! You're keeping her somewhere."

Mary slashes the air with the cane and growls.

"You don't know what you're talking about, you little brat."

"Oh, I suppose you've cut them out because you want something to read?" I say, waving my arms wildly. "And who are the toys for?"

"That's none of your business," she says, advancing on us.

"Please, Miss," says Star Kid. "Calm down. We're not here to hurt you."

"But I might hurt you," she says, slapping the cane across her palm. "I'm sick of the lot of you. Hanging out in front of my house, throwing things, calling me a witch."

"So you thought you'd kidnap one of us?" I say, the anger bubbling like lava. "Teach us a lesson? Well, Millie never hurt you! She never hurt anyone!"

And … I'm crying. Oh no, I'm crying. What am I doing? Superheroes don't cry. I try and fight it but that just makes it worse.

Star Kid clasps my shoulder while I desperately wipe my eyes. When my vision is clear, I look at Mary and see she's no longer pointing the cane.

"I don't have the girl," she says, softly this time. "I'd never do a thing like that. Truth be told, I had an argument with her father. A terribly rude man, and I got angry and cursed his family. So now I can't help but feel like it's my fault."

"But why do you have the clippings?" asks Star Kid.

"Look around you," says Mary. "Haven't you noticed I like keeping things? Whenever something happens in the news around here, I cut it out and keep it."

"And the toys under the stairs?" says Star Kid.

Mary sighs. Up close, I can see she has a row of white, wispy hairs on her chin.

"Like I told you before, it's none of your business," she says. "But if it will get you out of my house, I'll tell you."

Mary pokes the end of the cane into the carpet and leans on it. "I was a young lady once. You might find that hard to believe, looking at me now, but it's true. I was in love, too. Stanley, his name was. We were together since we were your age, probably. My first love. We lived in this house after we got married. It didn't look like this then. Stanley was very house proud. If he could see it now, he'd be horrified."

I can't help but wonder where this is going. At least I've stopped crying now.

"Stanley was in the army and he was sent overseas.

He'd been a few times and I learned to stop worrying so much. The last time he went, I found out I was expecting our baby. Oh, he was overjoyed when I spoke to him on the telephone. It was going to be a little girl; we both knew it. We didn't know it, but we knew it, if you know what I mean. So I couldn't help it. I went out and bought the little tea set and the doll's house. It was just like one I had when I was young. And I set it all up and the phone rang. I thought it was going to be Stanley again, and I was going to tell him all about it. But it wasn't. It was his sergeant. He'd been killed."

I watch a single tear roll down Mary's wrinkled face and I feel awful for making her relive this.

"I didn't cope with it," Mary goes on. "I've never learned to. People say time is a healer, but it's never healed me. There's just a big, gaping hole. And I know I'm trying to fill it with things, and I can't bear to throw anything out because of it, I know that, but it doesn't make it any easier. When my little girl was born, she was taken away. I couldn't look after her. I wasn't fit to care for a baby."

I glance across to Star Kid. His eyes are wet.

"I remember watching her in her cot from across the room. Her little fingers and toes moving. She looked just like Stanley and I couldn't stand it. I never saw her again."

Mary sniffs loudly. "I kept the toys in there all this time because I thought maybe one day she'd come and find me, and I'd show them to her. But she never did."

Mary stops talking. I have no idea what to say.

"We're sorry," says Star Kid. "From now on, we'll swing by at night and if we see anyone making a nuisance of themselves outside, we'll move them along."

Mary nods once. "Go on, then. Sling your hooks."

When we get outside, I can tell Star Kid wants to talk. "I know it's your sister, and I know you're scared, but please, from now on, calm down. We're lucky she didn't call the police back there."

I sit on the kerb and hold my head in my hands. I really thought I'd found her. Star Kid stays standing up. I see tiny spots of rain falling on the pavement, lit up by the lamp post.

"I have a question," says Star Kid.

"What is it?" I say, still not looking up.

"Why did you call yourself Damian back there?"

My skin prickles and my mouth goes dry. "Did I?"

"Yes."

The rain gets heavier. I feel it tapping on the top of my mask.

"It's … my nickname," I say.

There's a pause where it feels like he's trying to work out if I'm lying or not. "Your nickname is Damian?" says Star Kid.

"Yeah," I say. "Long story."

Worry Book

Tel doesn't buy the Damian nickname thing, I can tell.

CHAPTER 48

I keep thinking about Mary. How many times have I dismissed someone as being crazy without thinking about what might have happened to make them like that? I can't help but think about Mum. If we never find Millie, what will happen to her? Will she end up like Mary?

Looking at the news coverage was a mistake. It's not so much the stories but the comments underneath.

Why won't the parents show their faces? Something weird about that.

That estate is well dodgy. The police won't even go there, you know. That's why they have to have children dressed as superheroes patrolling it.

I want to sign up so I can argue back and tell

them they have no idea what they're talking about, but I stop myself. Like Tel says, I need to calm down. Getting angry won't bring Millie back. But what will?

Sharon walks in with some takeaway coffees from Gino's. When Dad sees the logo on the side of the cup, he pulls a face and doesn't drink it.

"They're having some kind of demo for Millie down at the community centre," says Sharon. "It's a nice thing to do, but we recommend you don't go, for obvious reasons."

"A demo?" asks Dad. "What's that going to achieve?"

Sharon shrugs. "It's just to show support, I think. Probably start a few new searches."

I'd checked Millie's fund earlier. It was up past ten thousand pounds. I wondered if Dad was going to pass any of that on to the people who were searching for her all day and all night.

"Never mind them, what are the police doing?" says Dad.

Sharon stays calm and professional, sitting next to Mum, who still stares at the Wall Bears, blankly.

"We're continuing our door-to-door enquiries in the wider area. I believe they're moving out to Gatesford this morning."

Dad stops pacing. "Oh yeah?" he says. "Why are they looking there?"

Sharon puts down her coffee. "It makes sense to cover as wide an area as possible, based on Millie's level of mobility and the amount of time that's passed."

"But you've had no reports from there, or anything like that?"

Sharon frowns a little. "Not that I know of."

Dad nods, then continues pacing. Weird.

I decide I'm going to this demo. I was up most of the night torturing myself, reading about kidnappers, and I found that often they will attend public vigils and things like that to take pleasure in the pain they've caused. I'm going to go and keep my eyes open for anyone acting weird.

When the time comes, I put on the only baseball cap I own and go downstairs. I keep my head down when I walk past the police parked outside, and don't turn straight towards the community centre, but take a long route round in case I'm being followed.

When I'm sure I'm alone, I head for the demo. There's a pretty big crowd gathered. I pull my hat down low. I don't want people asking me stuff.

There are lots of TV cameras there, filming what's

going on: the "FIND MILLIE" signs, the lit candles, the giant photos of her that they used on the news. I see Linda, Millie's day care teacher, dark rings around her eyes like she hasn't slept in days. I try to imagine what it would have been like if this had happened back at our old house. Would all our neighbours have come out like this? I don't know.

Life has changed around here, overnight. You don't see kids playing outside. With a child-snatcher on the loose, they're being kept inside. People would normally leave their windows open on warm nights, but not any more. I've seen people fitting extra locks to their doors, too.

Tel arrives and stands with me. "You know," he says, "if there's one good thing about this place, it's how we come together when bad stuff happens. I was only a little kid, but I remember people were great when Dad died." He sniffs. "I can't help but feel rotten about Mary, though. It feels like she's been shut out all these years over nothing. Maybe when we've found Millie – and we will, Phineas – we'll look for Mary's daughter."

There's a squeal of feedback as Pat stands on a crate and puts a loudhailer to her mouth. "Good afternoon, everyone. Thanks so much for joining us. You know why we're all here. One of our own has gone missing. Little Millie is a sweet girl and she needs to be home with her family."

I sense someone looking at me from the other side of the crowd. It's Gino. He gives me a thin smile and a nod. I return it.

"And we are never going to give up until she's found," says Pat.

The crowd bursts into cheering and applause. Millie's day care teacher is crying. Millie really loved going there. I spot something moving behind her. It's a man in a cap like mine. He looks kind of familiar.

"Everything all right?" Tel asks me.

I nod, but I'm trying to get a better look at this guy. His face is shielded by the shadow of the cap, and he has a black beard that seems out of place, but I know I've seen him somewhere before. I move away from Tel, keeping my eyes trained on him. I'm beginning to have a suspicion. A horrible suspicion.

"Uncle Shane?" I say under my breath. It is him, it really is. He's found us. For half a second, his eyes lock on to mine, then he turns and starts walking away from the crowd. My first thought is to run back to the flat and warn everyone, but if I do that, I'll lose him and he'll disappear again. I have to follow him.

"Finn, where are you going?" Tel calls after me.

"Wait there!" I tell him over my shoulder.

I don't have time to explain anything to Tel, not even to think: this may be the only chance I get to find Millie.

Shane cuts through the alley and heads along the cycle path. I can tell it's him from the way he walks: head down, hands shoved into his pockets. I walk along the path on the other side of the houses, keeping him in my sight each time I get to a gap. If I follow directly behind him I risk him turning around.

I try and silence the constant chatter in my brain and focus. I need to find out where he's staying. He seems to be walking in the direction of the bridge. There's a little hill in the middle of the street, so I run to the top and see him climbing the steps. I watch him until he is almost at the other side, then run down. I try and climb the stairs quickly but quietly as his head disappears down the other side. Where could he be going? How long has he been here? He goes past the petrol station and through the gates of the cemetery.

What? I hurry down the steps and get into the cemetery just as he's passing the war memorial in the middle. The cemetery has been searched loads of times. There's no way they'd have missed anything, is there? He passes Tel's dad's grave and heads for the gate at the other side. I haven't been this far before. Beyond the gate, there's a single street with about ten old-fashioned houses on it. I duck behind the tall hedge next to the gate and peep around the side. Shane stands outside number seven, looks around, then gets a key out, opens the door and walks in.

I know what I should do. I should run home and tell Sharon, or Dad, or anyone. But what I should do and what I am doing are two different things. What I am doing is running as fast as I can across the road to number seven and hammering the door.

It opens on the chain, and I see his eye peeping out at me.

"Let me in," I say.

He undoes the chain and there he is: Uncle Shane. He's grown a beard and he's shaved his head, but I can tell it's him: the broken front tooth, the narrow eyes, the crooked nose.

"Damian," he chuckles, like he's been expecting me. "Long time no see."

"Where is she?" It takes all my effort not to shake or let my voice wobble.

"Who?" he says.

"I'm not in the mood, Uncle Shane," I say. Damn. Why did I call him "Uncle"? "Just tell me what you've done with her."

Shane laughs and ruffles my hair. "Look at you, Damo. You're a big man, now."

I knock his hand away. "I just want to know where my sister is."

Shane rubs his chin, still smiling. "Remember when we went bowling? You, me and your dad? We both beat him, didn't we?"

"Just tell me where she is."

"And he was making excuses, wasn't he? 'Oh, the ball wasn't right. The finger holes were too big.'" Shane shakes his head. "Fact is, he's a loser. Always has been, always will be."

I go to speak, but he holds up a hand to silence me. "I don't have your little sister. Quite frankly, I'd love to know who did take her because I'd sort them out myself. You do not go after a man's kids, even if he is a snitch."

"So why are you here?" I say.

"Well, I've been trying to track your old man down for a while, and when the news broke about young Millie, the gods dropped him into my lap. I'm just here because I want to talk to him, that's all."

"What do you mean, talk to him?"

"I mean what I say. I want to talk to him. I haven't been able to yet because of all the police, but I know where he is now, and they can't stick around for ever." He tries to ruffle my hair again, but I step back. "You won't say anything, though. You're smarter than your dad. This is between him and me. It's up to you to make sure of that."

He watches me as I walk across the bridge back towards the cemetery, my legs trembling. Even when I'm at the other side, he's still there, on the doorstep.

The demo is still on when I get back to the estate, and I take the long way around so I can avoid Tel. I don't even look to see if he's still there. I don't have time to explain. I run up the stairs of Ambrose Court two at a time and when I finally burst through the door, I'm too out of breath to speak.

"Everything all right, love?" says Sharon.

Dad comes out of the kitchen, his phone in his hand. "What's up?" he says.

"It's … Uncle … Shane."

CHAPTER 49

The police sped straight round to number seven. Sharon stayed with us.

Mum woke up as much as the pills would let her. "Do you think he's got Millie?" she asked.

"I don't know," said Dad. "I wouldn't put anything past him, but try not to get your hopes up."

My phone buzzed with messages from Tel, but I couldn't concentrate on what they said. I needed to know that they'd got Uncle Shane.

I went to my room and lay on my bed, but I couldn't settle. I stood up and paced the floor. I stared out of the window. I picked up Millie's toys and turned them over in my hands. I thought back to the day she was born. I was so annoyed. I'd been the only one for the best part of ten years and, all of a sudden, someone else was going to be the centre of attention. But that all changed the first time I saw her. She was so cute, with those big brown eyes, and straight away I felt protective of her. Like I would stand in front of her and fight off anyone or anything. But I didn't. I wasn't there when she needed me.

Sharon's phone rang, so I quickly went into the lounge. When she hung up, I couldn't read her expression.

"Well, they've got him in custody," she said. "He was trying to escape when they arrived, so it's lucky you reported it when you did, Finn."

Dad squeezes my arm roughly.

"I'm afraid there is no sign of Millie, though," Sharon continued.

Mum clamped her hand over her mouth and started crying. As long as I live, I will never get used to that.

There's going to be a full search of the house and he will be questioned, but at the moment, there's no evidence he had her."

Dad cracked his knuckles and clenched his jaw. "We'll get her," he says. "Don't worry; we'll get her soon."

Later on, when Mum is in bed, I go to the kitchen

for a glass of water and Dad is sitting in the lounge with a beer. He's watching a film and doesn't even know I'm there. In the blue light from the TV, I can see he's smiling.

He's smiling.

Worry Book

What does he have to smile about?

CHAPTER 50

Mum has left the flat for the first time since Millie disappeared. Now Shane can't get to us, she's decided to show her face in public for the first time. They've set up a press conference at the community centre. Sharon has gone with her. They thought it would be best if Dad didn't go. He's gone out, though. He said to Sharon that the police are doing such a terrible job of searching for Millie that he's going to go and do it himself.

press

home. If you know anything, have seen anything, please come forward."

I can't watch any more. It's my fault Mum is like that.

I pick up the laptop and it opens to the funding page. I can see it updating in real time, the numbers jumping:

£19,851

£19,990

£20,005

It's going crazy. There are news articles linked to it at the bottom.

Still no sign of missing girl.

Police search house but find no trace of Millie.

"T....f...

CHAPTER 50

Mum has left the flat for the first time since Millie disappeared. Now Shane can't get to us, she's decided to show her face in public for the first time. They've set up a press conference at the community centre. Sharon has gone with her. They thought it would be best if Dad didn't go. He's gone out, though. He said to Sharon that the police are doing such a terrible job of searching for Millie that he's going to go and do it himself.

I put the news on. They're showing the press conference live. Mum looks so small up there, behind that table. Her voice is thin and wobbly as Sharon tries to encourage her to lean towards the mic so she can be heard over the clicking and whirring of the cameras.

"Please," she says. "We just want our little girl

home. If you know anything, have seen anything, please come forward."

I can't watch any more. It's my fault Mum is like that.

I pick up the laptop and it opens to the funding page. I can see it updating in real time, the numbers jumping:

£19,851

£19,990

£20,005

It's going crazy. There are news articles linked to it at the bottom.

Still no sign of missing girl.

Police search house but find no trace of Millie.

"Terrifying to think our kids could be snatched from their bedrooms," says Instagram star.

When I meet Star Kid on the roof of Primrose House, I'm shocked to see he doesn't have his mask on.

"Aren't you worried someone will see?"

"It's ten o'clock and we're on a roof," says Tel. "We'll be fine."

He looks at me, stone-faced. A bowling ball sized lump of dread presses down on my stomach. "What?" I say. "What's happened?"

Tel sits down and motions for me to do the same.

"Finn," he says. "I know."

The lump grows bigger. "You know what?"

"I know," he says again. "Damian."

It hangs in the air. He really does know.

"So many things make sense now," says Tel. "You calling yourself Damian in Mary's house, not wanting to be on camera, forgetting the name of your school!" He shakes his head with a disbelieving smile. "I knew there was something off then, but I couldn't figure it out."

I try to speak, but nothing comes out except a little croak.

"You want to know how I know?"

I nod.

"When you ran off at the demo, I went after you. I was worried about you. I wanted to be there in case you got yourself into trouble."

But I told him not to follow me. Then again, I was

331

so focused on following Shane, I wasn't really paying attention.

"I saw you talking to that man, but I stayed there after you went. I saw him loading things into his car and I went over, tried to ask him who he was, like I was just some kid from the neighbourhood. He told me to get lost, but I was just trying to stall him, because he seemed in such a hurry after talking to you. When the police arrived, I heard them say his name, so I did what anyone would do. I googled him. Guess what? He's a fugitive. Wanted for exactly the same things Ronnie was doing. The same things your dad was doing. And I dug deeper and deeper, until I found this website about gangsters. Ronnie wasn't on there, too small potatoes, probably. But Shane was, and there was a photo of him. And guess who he was standing next to? Your dad. Who is described as being in witness protection." He stops and shakes his head. "Why didn't you tell me?"

"That's why!" I manage to splutter out. "I couldn't! I'm literally not allowed to tell anyone."

"I know that," says Tel. "But when you entered into this thing, I thought it was understood that we trusted each other. Could tell each other anything."

"Yeah," I say. "And I do. Just not that."

Tel shakes his head, sadly. "Your dad is out doing collections again. But you probably knew that already."

I feel like I've been slapped across the face. "What? No, I didn't know that! He told us he was out looking for Millie."

Tel laughs, but there's no warmth to it. "You know what? There's something not right about this whole thing."

"What do you mean?" I say.

"Do you know how many child abductions we had round here before your family showed up? Zero. It has literally never happened before."

"What are you saying?"

Tel sighs. "I don't know what I'm saying. I don't know what to think any more."

"Look," I say. "I'm me. The person you know, Finn ... Phineas! *That's* me. I'm not pretending to be someone else. In fact, since putting on this costume, I've felt more me than I ever have in my whole life. I don't have to walk around having people being fake-nice to me because of who my dad is. I don't have some big man persona to live up to. This is me."

"How do I know you're telling the truth, though?"

he says, cutting me off. "You could be spinning me a line like you have been this entire summer."

How do I prove it to him? What am I supposed to say? Then, it comes to me.

"OK," I say. "I'm going to have it out with Dad again. But this time, I want you with me. There are no secrets any more. You know who he really is."

"Tomorrow?" says Tel.

"Tomorrow," I say. "I promise."

Worry Book

At this point it would be easier to write down things that I'm not worrying about.

CHAPTER 51

We head out in the early evening, suited-up. Dad left the flat half an hour ago. He said he was going on another search. Yeah, right.

Star Kid is quiet. He's looking at me differently, I can tell. I want to tell him that the person he's got to know over the past few weeks is the real me, but I can't find the words. For now, I need to focus on finding Dad.

You'd think, us being superheroes, that we'd have some kind of tracker, where we'd be able to pin him down to the millimetre, but we've got nothing. We stand outside each block and look up at the landings for signs of life. Every time a door opens, we get ready to pounce, only for it to be someone else.

"I think we should split up," I say.

"Oh, do you?" says Star Kid, sceptically.

"We'll keep in touch by phone," I say. "The second either of us sees him, we let the other one know."

Star Kid nods briskly. "Fine. I'll take the east side of the estate, from Ivatt Road onwards; you take everything on the other side."

We go our separate ways in search of Dad. The smells from George's chippy drift out of the air vents as I walk past, making my mouth water.

I walk along the streets, past posters of Millie and pink ribbons tied to lamp posts, and I look for Dad. Why would he be doing this again? With all the police around, too? It makes no sense. I'm almost at the bridge over the dual carriageway when my phone rings. It's Star Kid.

"I've got eyes on Daddy," he says. "Coming out of Swindale Court. Get here as soon as you can."

I turn and run the other way. Some kids congregated by the underpass cheer me on.

"Go and get 'em, Moon Boy!"

I will, I think. *I will.*

Another call.

"He's changed direction, heading for the precinct."

Why would he be going there? Does George still owe him money? That can't be right, can it?

"Don't approach him," I say to Star Kid. "Let me get there first."

When I get to the precinct, I find Star Kid by the chippy, taking little peeks around the corner.

"He's in Ali's shop," he says.

"Did you see him coming out of a flat?" I ask.

He nods. "Had his notebook in his hand."

I take a look around the corner. Ali's door opens and Dad walks out. Looks like he was just buying some stuff. He's got some washing-up liquid, a box of matches and … is that…?

"Cherry Zingas," I whisper.

I don't want to believe what I'm seeing, but it's true. He's bought a bag of Millie's favourite sweets. Maybe it's because he's missing her. Maybe he thinks it will make her easier to find, or something like that. He thinks he can coax her out of hiding with her favourite treat? It sounds insane, but I'm willing to believe anything right now.

Dad turns right and walks around the other side of the precinct towards the car park. I motion for Star Kid to turn and head the other way. We look around the corner and watch as Dad unlocks the car and gets in. Where is he going with those sweets?

He pulls the car out of the car park. No. I need to

follow him. A door opens and Gino walks towards his van.

"Hey!" I say.

Gino does a double take when he sees us. "Well, if it isn't the uncaped crusaders!"

"Can you give us a lift?" I ask.

He chuckles. "What, you don't have a Batmobile?"

"I'm serious," I say. "We need to go quick."

"What's going on?" says Star Kid.

"We need to get after him," I say.

"After who? Your da— I mean, that man you don't know?" says Gino.

I roll my eyes. "Gino knows," I explain to Star Kid. "He's known since I dropped my costume into his garden. Anyway, can we, please?"

"All right, get in," says Gino, nodding at the van.

We climb up to the front seats and squeeze in.

"Strap in, kids," says Gino. "The Nemesis at Alton Towers has got nothing on this bad boy."

Gino pulls the van out of the car park on to the main road. "I was actually on my way to the supermarket, but chasing someone is way more exciting. The only problem we have is, as you can see, I don't know where he's gone."

We sit at the junction. We can go left or right.

There's no sign of Dad's car either way. "Try right," I say.

"Aye aye, captain," says Gino, and turns the van on to the dual carriageway. "So, come on, then," he says. "You're going to have to tell me what's going on. Because right now, I feel like Batman's butler. What's his name? Albert?"

"Alfred," Star Kid says.

"Look, you know my dad isn't exactly what you'd call a nice person," I say.

"Well, you said it, not me," says Gino.

"He's been doing some bad stuff since we've been here," I say. "I thought he'd stopped, but he hasn't, and now … I don't even want to say what I think he's up to."

We drive on, but there's no sign of him anywhere. He must have absolutely gunned it.

"Do you have any idea where he might have gone?" asks Star Kid.

I think about it. Abbotsdale is out of the question: too posh. People around there don't need to borrow money from him. What other areas are there? Hold on. I think back to that day Sharon told us where the police would be searching. I remember Dad acting weird when she mentioned one of them. What was it called?

"Is there another estate around here?" I ask. "Gate something?"

"Gatesford," says Gino. "It's about five miles the other way."

"Can we go there, please?"

"Very good, Master Bruce," he says.

"You really need to broaden your horizons," says Star Kid.

Gino swings the van into a turning point and we start heading the other way, back past our estate, under the bridge, whizzing by the petrol station and the cemetery.

We pull into an estate that pretty much looks like ours. They have a precinct, too, but instead of a chippy, there's a Chinese takeaway. The houses and flats look similar, though.

"OK, we're here," says Gino. "Any ideas where to go now?"

"Could we just drive around for a bit?" I say.

My skin is prickling under my costume. I so badly want to be wrong, but at the same time, I want to be right.

"Wait!"

Gino slams the brakes on.

"Reverse a little bit."

Gino does as I ask him. There it is. Parked up at the end of a turning. Our car. "Down there," I say.

Gino manoeuvres the van and parks behind it.

There are two houses at this end of the street. One of them has all the curtains drawn. If I had to bet, I'd say he was in there.

"So, what's your old man up to?" says Gino.

"I don't know," I say. "But we're going to find out. You can leave us here if you want, Gino."

"No," he says. "I wouldn't feel right about that. Besides, the big Asda is open 'til eleven. I've got plenty of time."

A door in one of the other houses opens and a man shuffles out in a dressing gown and a pair of slippers. "Can I help you?" he says.

Star Kid, sitting closest to the door, winds the window down.

The bloke gawps at us. "Hang about, aren't you those superheroes?"

"Ten points to Gryffindor," says Star Kid.

"Has that car been there a lot?" I lean over and ask him.

"The red one?" he says. "Yeah, all the time – just lately."

"And the driver," I say. "Which house is

he visiting?"

"That one," says the bloke, pointing at the one with the curtains drawn. "Lord knows what he's doing in there with that weirdo."

"So who lives there?" I ask him.

"Johnny Clemons," says the bloke. "Right odd sort. I've never seen him open those curtains in all the years he's lived here. Knowing him, he probably owes the guy money."

I've heard enough. "Come on," I say to Star Kid. "We're going in."

Star Kid shuffles along and we get out.

"You boys want me to come with you?" Gino shouts out of the window, but I ask him to stay put.

"Is everything all right?" the bloke asks, nervously. "Not going to be trouble, is there?"

I don't answer because I don't know. I head up the path to the front door, with Star Kid behind me. I go to knock, but hesitate, my fist suspended in mid-air. Star Kid pats my back. "I'm with you, Moon Boy," he says.

I knock on the door. No response. I knock again, louder. Still nothing.

"Let's try around the back," I say.

We go around the side, stepping over an upturned

bin, a bucket full of cement and an abandoned rabbit hutch, to a garden almost as overgrown as Mary's. I peer into the kitchen. It's dirty and cluttered. I try the door, but it's locked. In the hallway beyond, a dim light comes from a single hanging bulb. I see a shape step in from another room. It's a man, but not Dad. He's small and bald. He sees us looking in through the window then suddenly runs up the stairs.

I kick at the door, but like the door to the public toilets on the night Millie went missing, it doesn't move. I have to get in. I can't explain it, but it feels like every second matters. There's a loose brick lying in the long grass. I run and pick it up. The brick smashes the glass and I put my hand through and open the door.

Inside, we crunch over the shards and I head for the stairs.

"Dad!" I yell. "Where are you?"

The man I saw in the hall comes to the top of the stairs. "Get out of here," he says in a trembling voice.

"Where's my dad?" I say.

"I don't know what you're talking about," he says. "I'm going to call the police."

"No, you're not," I say, walking up the stairs towards him.

There's a tiny part of my brain screaming at me, telling me I should be scared, but I'm not. Nothing is going to stand in my way. The man keeps telling me to stop, but I don't, and with every step we take, he panics more.

"I'm warning you," he says. "I'm warning you!"

On the top step, he wraps his arms around me and shoves me up the wall, but Star Kid sweeps his legs from under him and pins him to the floor.

"Dad!"

A door opens on to the landing and Dad steps out. He's smiling, but it's strained, his eyes are darting around.

"Relax!" he says. "Hey, mate, let Johnny up, please."

"Why should I?" Star Kid growls, digging him in the ribs with his elbow and making him yelp.

"Because we are going to discuss this like grown-ups," says Dad. "Now, please."

Star Kid digs in again, then stands up. Johnny climbs to his feet, looks at us, then at Dad, then back at us, then without a word, darts down the stairs and out the front door.

"Come on, then," I say. "Let's talk about it like grown-ups."

Dad chuckles. "Looks like neither of us are good

at keeping promises, are we?"

"Not really," I say. "Except me breaking my promises means I'm looking for Millie. You breaking yours means people getting hurt."

"Oh, listen to yourself," says Dad. "People getting hurt? You weren't bothered about that before. You were only too happy to take my money, then. Where did you get your conscience from?" I glance over at Star Kid and think about everything that has happened to get him to this point.

"I've always had it," I say. "I've just had some help bringing it out."

Dad laughs, all smug. "Oh, give it a rest, Damian."

I step forward, shoulders back, chin up, just like Tel showed me. "I'm not Damian any more. I'm Finn."

Dad doesn't say anything, just stands there in front of that door with his arms folded.

"Now," I say. "Where's Millie?"

Dad laughs. "How should I know?"

I try to push past him to get into that room but he stands in my way, solid. "What are you doing, Damian?" he says, using that low, menacing voice.

"Use. My. Proper. Name." I duck and, as fast and hard as I can, ram him in the stomach with my head, knocking him out of the way. I push my way in,

Star Kid behind me.

"Millie!" I shout. "Millie!"

There's a wooden dividing wall that looks like it was hastily put up. It's not right. Dad makes a grab for me, but Star Kid jumps on his back. Dad tries to throw him off, but Star Kid holds on tight.

"Hurry!" says Star Kid.

I push on the wall, looking for some sign of weakness; that's when I see a square in the bottom left-hand corner. It's probably half a metre wide. I get down on my hands and knees and push it. It moves.

"Stay out of there!" Dad yells.

I crawl inside. Dad breaks free and makes a grab for me, but it's too late. I'm in. It's dark in here. I can't see a thing. I feel around on the walls for a light switch. The flap opens and Dad's arm lunges in, making a grab for me. The light that spills in briefly illuminates a switch on the wall next to me, which I flick on.

There's a little bed, a TV and some books in here. And on the floor next to the bed, is a Santa Claus toy.

I'm crying. I can't help it, but I'm crying. I see a shape behind the bed, next to the wall.

"Millie?" I say. "It's OK. Finn's here."

Slowly, the shape moves. Behind me, Dad tries to

pull himself into the room, but the flap is too small for him and he's struggling. Millie's head pops up from behind the bed.

"Have we stopped playing hide-and-seek now?" she asks.

CHAPTER 52

We dodge Dad and get out of the room. I pick up Millie and run down the stairs, making for the front door. Dad comes after us, but he can't catch us. I'm quicker than I've ever been, stronger than I've ever been. I feel like nothing would be able to take me down.

I can hear Star Kid trying to get in Dad's way, but he's on my tail. When Gino sees us coming, he jumps out of his van.

"What the hell is going on here?" he says.

I don't answer and put Millie inside, shutting the door. "Lock it," I say to Gino.

Gino does as I ask him, then rounds on Dad. "Has she been in there the whole time?"

"Butt out. This doesn't concern you," says Dad.

"That's where you're wrong, mate. Natasha is my employee and my friend and she is at her wits' end."

"I said, butt out!" Dad roars.

Star Kid stands next to me, forming a protective wall in front of the van. Dad runs his hands down his face.

"I did this for us, Damian," he says.

"I'm fed up of hearing that," I say. My stomach is surging with sickness and it takes all my effort not to throw up. "All that stuff you've done? It wasn't for us and you shouldn't try and put it on us. It was all you."

"That estate's not for us," he says. "We don't belong there. You've seen that fund? Another week and we'd have enough to buy a new house, anywhere you like. And doing this drew Shane out of his hiding place! We'll never have to worry about him again!"

"Those people donated that money to help find Millie," says Star Kid. "You conned them."

"I was doing the best thing for my family," he says.

"Have you seen Mum this past week?" I say. "How can this be the best for her?"

"It's only short term," says Dad. "Once we're out of that place, she'll be fine."

"Are you kidding me?" I say. "It's over, Dad."

Dad laughs, a crazed, desperate cackle. "No, it isn't! Look, we can get in that car right now: you, me and Millie. We'll go and get Mum and we'll be away. Fresh start."

I shake my head. "Everybody back in the van."

"Damian, no." Dad puts a hand out to stop me, but I bat it away.

"My name is Finn," I say.

Gino unlocks the van and I climb in. Behind me, there's a thud as Dad tackles Gino for the keys, jumping in after me. I scratch and claw at him, but he pushes me aside and gets into the driver's seat.

Millie screams as we screech out of the road, bumping and scraping our own car on the way.

"Stop the van, Dad," I yell. "This is stupid."

"Just put your seat belts on, both of you," he barks over the roar of the engine.

Dad spins the van on to the dual carriageway, throwing me against the door. I fasten Millie into the middle seat, then myself into the other. The way Dad is driving, we'll end up going through the windscreen.

"Where do you think you're going?" I say, trying to stop my voice wobbling. "You can't seriously think you're going to escape?"

Dad swerves into the other lane and a lorry blasts its horn at us. "That's exactly what I'm going to do. All of us. We'll go into the countryside. Hide out for a few days. Then your mum will come to us. After that, it's just a case of getting a boat over to France. Then we're clear. All that money will set us up for a bit."

I grab Millie's hand and hold it as tight as I can. I'm trying to let her know it's going to be all right, even if I don't believe it.

The siren starts off quiet but is soon a scream. I twist around to see two police cars right behind us now.

"You've got to stop the van, Dad. Please."

Dad laughs. "You think this is the first time I've had police after me? Where's your Butcher fighting spirit, Damian?"

"My name is Finn," I say again. "And if this is the Butcher fighting spirit, I don't want it."

But Dad's not listening, I can tell. There's a turning up ahead. A sharp one. I know what he's thinking.

"Hold on tight, kids."

With one arm, I pull Millie close, and with the other, I hang on to the handle above the door as the force of the sudden turn lifts us out of our seats. And there's another lifting feeling, too. I look out of the window and see the van is tilting. Oh no. Oh no, we're going to tip over. I hold Millie even tighter and screw my eyes shut but then *BANG*, the tyres hit the ground again and we're carrying on.

Dad yelps with wild laughter. The police didn't make the turn. We're alone again. Dad yanks the van around a slow-moving car and a van coming the other way has to brake to avoid hitting us.

"Daddy, I'm scared!" says Millie.

Dad reaches across and pats Millie's leg as he steers. "No need to be scared, baby. Daddy's taking you somewhere safe."

"Is that what you said when you kidnapped her?" I spit back, but Dad doesn't reply.

On the far side of the road, there's a thick wood, and call it the Butcher instinct if you want, but I know exactly what Dad is going to do. As quietly as I can, I pull my phone off my belt and hold it next to the door where Dad can't see it. Looking straight ahead, I scroll to the maps app and open it. When it loads our location, I take a screenshot, then hit share, followed by the first name on my suggested contacts.

"What are you doing on that thing?" Dad snaps, looking over at me.

Oh no. I thought I was being careful.

"Give it to me," he snaps, quickly beckoning with his spare hand.

I go to do as he says, but then I stop and secure the phone back in my belt. "No."

"Don't get smart, Damian, it's not the time," Dad warns.

"I said no," I say, keeping my voice as steady as I can.

Dad swings the van down a dirt track into the woods. He keeps driving until the sky is blocked out by a canopy of trees, then he pulls off the road and parks the van by a bush.

"I reckon we've lost them," he says. "Now we wait here for a while until the coast is clear."

This probably isn't the first time Dad has used this method to hide from the police. I can tell from the way it came so naturally to him. Dad leans over Millie and holds out his hand.

"Come on: phone. Don't make me ask again."

I glance out of the window and, through the gloom, see water glimmering. It's about fifty metres away. I squint harder and make out more of it. It stretches far away, until the trees completely block it out. I work it out and realize it must be the lake, the same one we hired the boat at.

I don't wait for Dad to ask again. I know exactly what I've got to do. I squeeze Millie's knee, whisper "Be brave" to her, then open the door and run.

Dad shouts my old name and jumps out after me, chasing me around the van. He's left his door open. Yes! Without stopping for even a second, I reach in and grab the keys out of the ignition.

"What do you think you're doing?!"

I know what I'm doing. I zip across the front of the van and run for the lake. Dad is behind me. My legs pump harder as I duck in and out of the trees. I feel a swoosh in the air behind me, which must be Dad's hand. He's close, but so is the lake. I can smell the water and the mud.

Dad's hand hits my back, but my rubber suit makes me too hard to grab. I jump over a fallen tree and hear a thud behind me. Dad must not have made it, but I haven't got time to turn around. I'm nearly at the lake now.

Something has my leg. I slam to a halt and grab a tree trunk to stay upright. I hope it might just be a vine or a root I'm tangled in, but I look down and see Dad's hand around my ankle.

"Give me the key, Damian," he grunts between

354

short breaths.

"For the last time," I say, "MY. NAME. IS. FINN!"

I launch the key through the last few trees, looping it high into the sky, before it plops into the lake. Dad jumps to his feet and runs to the edge of the water, but it's too far in.

Dad rounds on me, his face flushed red, spit flying everywhere.

"Why did you do that, you little idiot?"

I laugh when I remember what Tel said about the *Wizard of Oz*. He really is the pathetic old man behind the curtain.

"You told me I had to learn to stand up for myself," I say. "Looks like I have."

Dad must hear the police car door close, because he tries to run. He doesn't get far, though. There are too many of them. Tel must have shown them my text.

I can't watch as they handcuff him and bundle him into the car. I find Millie and we hug.

"You're a brave super-duper hero," she says.

I don't feel brave, though. I'm more scared than I've ever been in my life. It's just the three of us now.

CHAPTER 53

It's been two weeks since we found Millie. It's been rough. Dad is the most hated person in the country, his face on the front page of every newspaper every day, and when they found out about his past, it only got worse. One paper even suggested that Mum was in on it.

Thankfully, everyone around the estate has been brilliant. They've brought presents for Millie and they've defended us against some horrible reporters. A video of Ali telling a journalist from the paper that said bad stuff about Mum to sling his hook went viral.

Gino comes around most nights and makes us dinner. It's always delicious and always fun. Still, I know some dinners with Dad were fun too and when

356

I think of him in prison, I want to cry, and I'm trying to remember that I shouldn't feel bad for stopping him, but I still do.

People who donated to Millie's fund will be able to get their money back, and any money that isn't claimed is going to go to the food bank at the community centre. Dad would hate that.

I'm sitting on the roof of the underpass with Star Kid, our legs dangling above the cycle path. We're pretty famous now, too. "Real life Avengers bust kidnapper!" was the front page headline the day after it happened.

"So what now?" says Star Kid.

"Thinking of branching off. Starting my own superhero group," I say.

"You are not," says Star Kid, slapping my shoulder.

I nod solemnly. "I've already recruited Pat and Ali as my sidekicks. Pat says we can use the community centre as our official headquarters. All the squash we can drink."

Star Kid sighs. "I can't compete with that."

We sit quietly for a few minutes in the late afternoon sun. Soon, we'll be starting school again and who knows how that's going to go? But right now, I'm just enjoying being with my friend.

"So, I take it you're definitely not moving away, then?" Star Kid breaks the silence.

Our solicitor had explained to us that with Dad sure to be in prison for a very long time, we have the option of moving away and starting again with different identities. We thought about it for a while, but none of us could face all of that again. Besides, if we moved, I'd never get to see Tel again.

I shake my head. "No way."

Star Kid smiles, reaches across and holds my hand, his fingers firmly gripping my palm. "Well, good. I mean, for one thing, I'd have to find someone else who'd be willing to wear that costume. Not sure it would be an easy sell, after such a hot summer…"

"Fair point," I say.

"Look." Star Kid nods up the cycle path towards Mary's house. "I think that's them."

There's a woman and a man approaching.

"I wonder what she's going to think when she sees the house," I say.

"I think she'll get it," says Star Kid. "She knows Mary has had a hard life since she lost her."

The door opens and Mary walks up the path. She's wearing different clothes. They look almost new. The two women face each other for a second. It looks like they're talking, but I can't tell what they're saying. Then, the woman holds out her arms and they hug.

Star Kid cheers and claps quietly, so only we can hear. He's been working on this obsessively, tracking down Mary's daughter.

"I'm telling you, Phineas," he says. "This thing we do, it's magic."

And as I look at Mary and her daughter, meeting for the first time since she was a baby, then over their heads at Ambrose Court in the background, where I'm pretty sure Mum, Millie and Gino are sitting around the kitchen table, playing Junior Monopoly and letting Millie win, I think I agree.

Acknowledgements

Many thanks for reading! This book will always be a special one for me, because I started it during lockdown and it kept me sane during those long months of isolation, anxiety and Zoom quizzes.

Thanks as ever to my agent Penny Holroyde for her guidance in the book's early stages and for finding it a wonderful home. Speaking of which, thanks to everyone at Scholastic, especially Linas Alsenas for his invaluable editorial input. The book has my name on the cover, but so many more people have worked on it and shaped it into the thing of beauty you have in your hands, so shout-out to them.

I'd be remiss if I didn't thank my family for their patience while I pecked away at this manuscript and stared into space trying to resolve plot holes. Hester and Dougie: you're my bestest friends in the whole world and I promise never to turn to a life of crime. Unless it pays really well, obviously.

Before I go, I thought I'd say a big thanks to my day job colleagues at Royal Mail Tamworth. You all inspire me more than you know. Right.